"Years ago my daughters and wife were inhaling Robin Gunn's stories and loving them, so I had to take a peek myself to find out why. I did. Robin's characters are believable, and her stories have just the right blend of hope, broken hearts, disappointments, lighthearted fun, joy, and an eternal perspective. The Lord Jesus always plays a role, whether behind the scenes or in the thick of things. Robin lives the faith that's so evident in her books. She knows how to tell a story—and the stories she tells make an eternal difference."

RANDY ALCORN, AUTHOR OF *DEADLINE*

"When you read a Robin Gunn book, you know you're going to receive a tender lesson in what it means to belong to Christ—and you will be blessed for it."

FRANCINE RIVERS, AUTHOR OF *REDEEMING LOVE* AND
THE MARK OF THE LION SERIES

"Robin's warmth, insight, and humor spill over from her heart onto the written page. She delights us with the well-woven fabric of a well-told tale, and I'm certain Robin delights the Lord with her obvious passion for Him."

PASTY CLAIRMONT, AUTHOR OF *GOD USES CRACKED POTS* AND
SPORTIN' A 'TUDE

"Robin Jones Gunn cares. She cares about her characters, she cares about her readers, and most of all, she cares about their mutual search for a life that pleases the Lord. Her novels are a delight to read—perfectly crafted, heartwarming, and fun. I'm always thrilled when one of Robin's books appears on the top of my to-be-read stack!"

LIZ CURTIS HIGGS, AUTHOR OF *MIXED SIGNALS, BOOKENDS,* AND
BAD GIRLS OF THE BIBLE

"Whenever I think of stories that touch the heart, I think of Robin Jones Gunn's. They touch my heart and leave me wanting more. Reading a novel by Robin Jones Gunn is like spending time with a good friend…troubles are lighter and joys are deeper."

ALICE GRAY, AUTHOR OF STORIES FOR THE HEART
BOOK COLLECTION

"Robin Jones Gunn writes from a heart of love. Her tender stories honor the Savior and speak truth to a world desperately eager to hear it."

ANGELA ELWELL HUNT, AUTHOR OF *THE TRUTH TELLER*

"Robin Gunn is a gifted and sincere storyteller who gets right to the heart of matters with her readers."

MELODY CARLSON

D1051937

THE GLENBROOKE SERIES

Wildflowers

ROBIN JONES GUNN

Multnomah®Publishers *Sisters, Oregon*

WILDFLOWERS
published by Multnomah Publishers, Inc.
© 2001 by Robin's Ink, LLC

International Standard Book Number: 1-59052-239-7

Cover design and images by Steve Gardner/His Image PixelWorks
Edited by Janet Kobobel Grant

Scripture quotations are from:
The Holy Bible, King James Version

Holy Bible, New Living Translation (NLT) © 1996. Used by permission of
Tyndale House Publishers, Inc. All rights reserved.

New American Standard Bible (NASB) © 1960, 1977 by the Lockman Foundation

The Holy Bible, New King James Version (NKJV) © 1984 by Thomas Nelson, Inc.

New Revised Standard Version Bible (NRSV) © 1989 by the Division of Christian
Education of the National Council of the Churches of Christ
in the United States of America

The Holy Bible, New International Version (NIV) © 1973, 1984 by International
Bible Society, used by permission of Zondervan Publishing House

Multnomah is a trademark of Multnomah Publishers, Inc.
and is registered in the U.S. Patent and Trademark Office.
The colophon is a trademark of Multnomah Publishers, Inc.

Printed in the United States of America

For information:
MULTNOMAH PUBLISHERS, INC.•P. O. BOX 1720•SISTERS, OREGON
97759

Library of Congress Cataloging-in-Publication Data:
Gunn, Robin Jones, 1955-
    Wildflowers / by Robin Jones Gunn. p.cm. ISBN 1-57673-631-8
                                                         1-59052-239-7
    1. Separated people–Fiction. 2. Restaurateurs–Fciction.
    3. Restaurants–Fiction. I. Title.
    PS3557.U4866 W55 2001 813'.54–dc21 2001003457

04 05 06 07 08—10 9 8 7 6 5 4

For my sister-in-law, Kate Gunn Medina,
who for more than twenty-five years
has bestowed generously on me
love and friendship.
You are a treasure.

"I was asleep, but my heart was awake."

SONG OF SONGS 5:2, NASB

Chapter One

Genevieve was dreaming. She knew she was dreaming because this was the third—no, the fourth—time the same dream had invaded her sleeping mind. The dream always started the same way: She was standing inside her newly acquired Wildflower Café, looking out the window at all her Glenbrooke friends who had gathered to celebrate the grand opening. She was ready to open the door and let them in when she paused. Scanning the smiling faces, she searched for her husband, Steven. But Steven wasn't there.

Steven was never there.

Pressing her eyelids tighter, Genevieve gripped the edge of her dream world and held her breath, willing herself not to wake up. She desperately wanted a new ending to this dream, a conclusion that was different from the way this scene had ended in real life.

A little more than two months ago, when Genevieve stood inside the Wildflower Café the same way she now stood in her dream, the phone had rung. Steven was calling to say he was stuck in Chicago. Heavy snowfall had delayed all flights that day, and he wouldn't be able to fly out until the next morning. She told him she understood. She said she didn't hold it against him.

Yet in her subconscious she kept returning to that moment, waiting in her dream for the phone to ring. This time she would tell him what she really thought. She would let herself cry and tell him it wasn't okay for him to be stuck in Chicago. The snow wasn't a good enough excuse. He had done this to her one too many times.

Genevieve knew that in dreams people could fly on rocket ships or clouds or with wings they had suddenly sprouted. Snowflakes could turn into giant soap bubbles. In dreams, even a weary airline pilot could ride all the way to Glenbrooke inside one of those magic soap bubbles and arrive at the front door of the café at just the right moment.

With all her might, she tried to make the desired ending come to her in her dream. But it was no use. Her dream cut off, as it always did, like a broken reel of a home movie. Once again she was stuck in the darkness, hoping against hope that she could rethread the puddle of dream film gathered at her feet and start up the unresolved scene in her subconscious one more time. But it didn't work. She was stuck.

Genevieve opened her eyes and drew in a deep breath. *Get over it, Genevieve. Let it go. This is the way things are.*

She blinked, trying to adjust her eyes to the bedroom's

ROBIN JONES GUNN

darkness. On the rooftop of their warm home pattered the persistent Oregon spring rain. Beside her, Steven slept.

Steven Ahrens, the steady airline captain who had swept Genevieve up into his life more than twenty years ago slept soundly, as he always did. He lay on his back with his left arm above his head and his right arm on his chest. In the faint glow from the digital alarm clock, Genevieve watched her husband's frame as each unhurried breath came after the other. In his sleeping and in his waking, Steven lived his life at a predictable, unruffled pace. Routine was everything. And everything was routine.

Genevieve listened as the rain tapped on the window. She thought about how she had hoped their life would be different when they moved to Glenbrooke. Opening the Wildflower Café was possibly the biggest event in her life, aside from giving birth to their three daughters. Why couldn't Steven have been there with her at the grand opening? Why did she continue to coax a different ending out of her subconscious? She couldn't change the past.

Fluttering on the edge of sleep, Genevieve told herself she didn't want to change everything about the past. Half awake, half asleep, she hovered over a reflecting pool of memories. Her heart had flown often to this familiar place where the earliest images of her love for Steven glistened with pristine clarity and beckoned her to draw closer.

In her mind's eye, Genevieve saw herself swimming in Lake Zurich on that brilliant summer afternoon so many years ago. She was eighteen on the outside and perhaps younger than that in her heart. Her slim frame emerged from the brisk water, and she hurried to the towel she had left on the grass beside her girlfriends. The towel was there, but her friends were gone.

Standing on the corner of her towel was a fair-skinned young man who asked in very poor French if she knew the time. His build was medium and muscular. His fine, short hair was combed straight back. He had a perfectly straight nose that topped the *O* he formed with his lips like an exclamation point.

Genevieve guessed he was American and answered him in English. His face warmed with a shy, grateful expression. He took off his sunglasses, revealing deep blue eyes, blue like the sky above the clouds. He smiled at her, and Genevieve was smitten.

The memory shifted to a sidewalk café only five blocks from Lake Zurich where Steven was trying his first taste of raspberry strudel with heavy cream. Genevieve wore a pale yellow summer dress and sipped a demitasse of Turkish coffee. Wisps of her thick, brown hair danced across her forehead as she sat across from this fascinating, twenty-four-year-old man, and she used her well-practiced English to tell him what it was like to grow up in Zurich.

His steady eyes seemed to memorize every detail of her face. He listened to her with an expression that said, "You are the most captivating woman I've ever met. Ask anything of me, and I'll do it."

What she asked of him, without a single word, was for her first kiss. What he gave her with that kiss was a kingdom. His kingdom. His life. And into the life of this soft-spoken man with the warm, steady gaze, Genevieve contentedly had tucked herself like granulated sugar folded into a bowl of whipped-up egg whites.

Now, in the sanctuary of their bedroom, Steven turned toward her in his sleep. His straight nose was only inches from her as his steady breath fluttered over her eyelids. She was so close to him yet Genevieve was so far away. Even the memories of their love's first awakening brought no warmth to her spirit. All the doors to her heart were shut, and all the shades were pulled down tight.

When Genevieve entered the back door of the Wildflower Café at seven-thirty that morning, she felt weary from all the wrestling she had done in the night. She noticed that a few slender sunbeams had managed to slip past the heavy rain clouds. The sunbeams blazed their way through the window above the large kitchen sink, warming her forearm as she washed her hands. Perhaps Glenbrooke would have some sunshine today after all. It made her feel hopeful.

Leah Edwards, Genevieve's assistant, charged through the swinging door from the dining room with her usual energy. "Hey, good morning! I didn't expect you this early."

"Steven is taking the girls to school. I thought I'd start on the brownies."

Leah's short blond hair was tucked under a baseball cap, which was her favorite substitute for a chef's hat. When Genevieve catered Leah and Seth's wedding six months ago, a fast friendship formed between the two women. Genevieve soon discovered that she would never have been able to make this dream café a reality if it hadn't been for Leah's choice to leave her former career at the hospital and join her.

"Has it been busy?" Genevieve quickly dried her hands and pulled an apron over her head.

"No, just the regulars. Oh, and someone who wants to see you. He's at table four."

"Who is it?" The only opening from the kitchen to the dining room was a swinging door, so Genevieve couldn't see who was at table four.

"He said his name was Richard Palmas. He wants to interview you." Leah popped two slices of rye bread into the toaster.

"Interview me? Why?"

Leah flipped two fried eggs on a plate and handed it to Genevieve, motioning for her to include the toast. "He's writing a book on great cafés of the Northwest. I'm guessing he wants to include the Wildflower in his book. Here, these eggs are for Dr. Norton. And don't butter the toast. I'll cover the kitchen while you go meet Mr. Palmas."

Genevieve delivered the breakfast, greeted an elderly couple at table seven, and warily made her way to table four. A middle-aged man in a black, V-necked sweater and jeans greeted Genevieve with expressive eyes.

"Would you like more coffee?" she asked.

"No thanks. You must be Genevieve. I'm Richard Palmas. How are you this morning?"

"Fine." Genevieve noticed that he had been taking detailed notes.

"Did your associate tell you I'm writing a book on the best cafés in the Northwest?"

"Yes."

"When would be a good time for me to ask you a few questions?"

"Around nine o'clock would be good. It usually slows down then."

Richard glanced at the eight unhurried customers in the small café. Raising an eyebrow, he said, "Is this your morning rush?"

"Yes. Such as it is." Genevieve felt her neck warming. "This is our morning rush."

"Then I will take another cup of coffee," Richard said. "And some breakfast while I wait."

"I'll bring you a menu," Genevieve said.

"No." Richard touched her arm lightly before she could slip away. "I don't need a menu. Bring me whatever you would consider your house specialty."

Genevieve smiled tentatively. She hoped he couldn't tell how uncomfortable she felt. "Does an omelet sound good to you?"

Richard tilted his head and gave her a confident grin. "Sure. Make it the best omelet on your menu."

Genevieve slipped back into the kitchen, thankful for a place to hide. "Are you ready to switch places?" she asked Leah.

"Sure. I went ahead and mixed up the brownies, but I haven't started the soup yet. The broccoli is in the sink. Do you know if we have any more decaf tea bags? I couldn't find any this morning."

"I'll check on it. Anything else?"

Leah balanced two plates on her left arm. "Did I tell you yesterday about the fan over the stove? It keeps turning off and on. It might be a short. I left it off all morning."

"Okay, I'll have it checked."

Leah slid into the dining room with a the pancakes while Genevieve gave her thick, brown hair a twist and secured it with a clip at the back of her head. *Don't let yourself feel intimidated by this man. It's only an omelet. You've made hundreds of omelets before.*

As omelets go, the bacon, cheese, and mushroom omelet Genevieve prepared was respectable. Not award-winning, but certainly respectable. Leah served the omelet to Mr. Palmas while Genevieve made the broccoli cheese soup and cooked the other breakfast orders. Nine o'clock arrived, and only three customers, who were finishing their morning coffee, remained. Genevieve turned the kitchen over to Leah. She decided to leave on her white apron and walk into the dining room as if Richard Palmas were any other Glenbrooke customer.

It would have worked except that from the moment she entered the dining room, he seemed to be scrutinizing her every move.

"I heard you grew up in Switzerland," Richard said before she had a chance to sit down.

"Yes."

"And you lived in Pasadena before moving here a year ago."

Genevieve nodded.

"I also heard you're married to a commercial airline pilot."

"That's right."

"Interesting. You must travel a lot."

"No, not very much. We have three daughters. Our oldest is in college now, but the other two keep me close to home since Steven is gone so much of the time." Genevieve adjusted her position on the chair and chided herself for divulging so much personal information. She tried to redirect the questions to the café. "How was your omelet?"

"Better than most."

What was that supposed to mean?

"Did I hear correctly that the café is closed on Sundays?"

"Yes, our hours are seven to four on weekdays and eight to two on Saturdays."

"No dinners then, only breakfast and lunch."

"That's right. Only breakfast and lunch." Genevieve noticed how hard her chair felt. A cushioned pad would make a world of difference. She noticed, too, that the round table at which they sat was too large for them to have a quiet conversation. She felt as if she had to speak louder than she liked to be heard over the heater's hum and the echoing clatter of dishes in the kitchen.

"How long have you owned the café?"

"About two months."

"I imagine you have plans to make additional changes."

"Yes, well…we have some ideas, but…" Genevieve felt her throat tightening. The only changes she had been able to afford were the sturdy tables and chairs that replaced the wornout tables and vinyl booths. She still was working on putting up new pictures to cover the walls where baskets of faded artificial flowers had once hung. It was the best she could do with her budget. She wasn't about to admit to this stranger, or anyone else, that the café had come nowhere near breaking even during the last two months.

Richard closed his notebook and looked at Genevieve with his mesmerizing, green eyes. "I'll be honest with you, Genevieve. I would like very much to include your café in my book, but I think I've come prematurely. Could I return in a couple of months? I'd like to see you again—that is, I'd like to see what you've done by then. I think your rating will be higher once you've had a little more time to settle in."

Genevieve drew in a deep breath and tried to sound calm. "I appreciate your interest in the café. However, I can't guarantee that things will be much different in a few months. You might save yourself some time if you left this café out of the book."

Richard seemed humored by her direct response. "More is involved in such a decision than you might think. You see, my publisher requires that I include a café from this area. Each region needs to be represented, and as you may know, very few cafés are left around here. That is, cafés that would qualify for what I'm after."

He leaned closer, across the too-wide table. "The location of this café is perfect for tourists, especially with the antique store that opened up at the end of Main Street. I considered including this café several months ago when I started to collect information for the book. But my first visit here last fall was pretty discouraging. I had hoped that with all you have going for you, as well as your European background, you might be the one to finally bring some sparkle to this place."

Genevieve parted her lips, but no response found its way out. *Was I just insulted? Or is this man politely challenging me to make something more of the café?*

"I'll be back in a few months." Richard stood and reached for his raincoat. "When I return, feel free to dazzle me."

With that, he turned and walked out the door.

Genevieve stayed in her uncomfortable chair and watched Richard Palmas stride past the front window.

"How did the interview go?" Leah came over and leaned against the table.

"It went," Genevieve said flatly.

"Is that good or bad?"

"I don't know. He said he's coming back in a few months, after we have a chance to settle in more."

"That's good," Leah said. "Have you read any of his books?"

"No." Genevieve didn't like the way he had mixed all her feelings into a swirl. Especially when she had so little energy left for emotions of any kind.

"He's pretty well known," Leah said. "I didn't know who he was, but Brad was in here earlier, and he recognized him. Brad said that Richard Palmas has a line of books called *All the Best*. He writes a column with that same name for a newspaper in Seattle. His books have a rating system for the hotels and restaurants he evaluates. Brad said one of his 'best' ratings can make your business fly and one of his 'worst' ratings can break you."

"Well." Genevieve rose and pushed in her chair. "We don't need his evaluation to make our business fly. Our customers are all local. They aren't going to stop coming here just because someone from Seattle says our desserts are great but our chairs are uncomfortable, which they are, by the way."

Leah said, "Hold that thought." She slipped over to the register to help one of the customers.

Genevieve stepped over to the chair where Mr. Palmas had been sitting. She lowered herself with a Goldilocks sort of test in mind. Yes, the chair was too hard. It was just as uncomfortable as her chair had been.

Why didn't I ever notice this before? I guess I never sat out here for very long. Why haven't the customers complained?

Genevieve knew the answer. These were loyal locals who stopped in every day. Some of them would come for their morning coffee even if they had to stand in the corner because there were no chairs.

People don't take their time here. They run in and run out. If we could get some cushions on these chairs, the customers might linger and order dessert. That would push up our profits.

Purging her mind of Mr. Palmas and his supposedly powerful evaluation, Genevieve set her thoughts on improving the café. This was one area where her emotions were still free to soar.

I have to find a way to turn things around. I can only draw from the café bank account a few more months before I'll have to admit defeat. And if I admit defeat here, what will that mean about the rest of my life?

Chapter Two

The next morning the alarm went off at five o'clock as scheduled. Steven rose and headed for the shower, scuffing his bare feet on the carpet as he always did.

Genevieve rolled over in bed and tried to remember what day it was. All she remembered was that Steven was flying to Singapore today, and ten days later he would be back in her everyday life. For the next ten days she would live the other life she lived when he was gone. She would make all the decisions and handle all the details the way she had all these years. She would revert to being a part-time single parent.

For more than two decades, Genevieve had lived with this routine, yet something inside her had failed to settle into quiet acquiescence to Steven's schedule. A silent hurt and anger came over her, as it always did. She knew that she could give him a home and children and even herself. But she couldn't give Steven the world.

And he wanted the world. He wanted to travel. He loved his job.

Genevieve chased away her wounded feelings with a harsh rebuke. She had a good life and no real reason to complain.

Reaching for her yellow fleece robe and nuzzling her bare toes into a pair of fur-lined moccasins, Genevieve made herself get out of bed. She pulled her hair back in a clip and headed for the kitchen where she made coffee. The "recipe" for Steven's coffee hadn't changed in twenty-six years: half French roast, half decaf espresso with three shakes of cinnamon on top of the grounds before brewing.

Genevieve yawned and opened the kitchen window shade. The persistent spring rain flung itself against the glass as it had every morning for the past three days.

Genevieve thought of the riddle her youngest daughter, Mallory, had asked at the dinner table the night before. "If April showers bring May flowers, what do May flowers bring?"

Steven had grinned. "I know." He turned to their middle daughter. "Do you know, Anna?"

Anna shook her shoulder-length, caramel-colored hair. At fourteen, she couldn't be bothered with riddles.

"Pilgrims!" Steven declared. "Mayflowers bring pilgrims. Is that right, Mallory?"

"How did you know?" Mallory turned her large brown eyes toward Steven with undying affection.

Genevieve thought about how all three of their daughters idolized Steven. In the back of her mind echoed the reminder that she was the one who had been there through the teething, chicken pox, and soccer practices. She was the one who had balanced the checkbook, managed the carpools, mowed the lawn, and baked the birthday cakes. But Steven was the one they adored.

He appeared in the kitchen just then, breaking her thoughts. He looked handsome in his pilot's uniform with his hat in one hand and pulling his wheeled suitcase with the other.

"Your coffee is ready." Genevieve reached for his travel mug.

"You're wonderful," Steven said. "Thanks. I'll call you in a few days." He kissed her lips once then kissed her again with a lingering sweetness. "I love you," he murmured. "I always have loved you, and I always will."

"I know," Genevieve answered routinely. "Be safe on the roads. It's still raining."

"I will. *Ciao, mon ami.*"

The door into the garage closed with a thud. All that remained of Steven was a whiff of his leather-scented after-shave and a hint of cinnamon rising from the coffeemaker. A familiar, sickening thought paraded itself through Genevieve's mind. *What if he doesn't come home this time? What if my unresponsiveness pushes him away for good?*

With determination she shoved the thought aside. She had enough to worry about without imagining dramatic endings to her marriage. She knew she had closed up her heart the way a summer cabin is closed for the winter. Deep down, she hoped that spring would come again. The ice would thaw, and she would thoroughly clean her heart's dark corners.

But not today. Today the issue dominating her thoughts was how she could keep her fledgling business alive. The challenges in her marriage would have to wait until later. Today she had a café to run.

Snapping into her routine, Genevieve poured herself a large mug of cherry almond tea and trotted upstairs to take a hot shower. A brisk tidying up of the master bathroom became the antidote to this morning's melancholy.

She woke Anna and Mallory, made oatmeal, signed the permission form for Mallory's field trip; and then dropped the girls off at their schools.

Genevieve turned down Main Street and was about to pull around to the back of the Wildflower Café, as she always did, and park in the gravel lot behind the kitchen. But suddenly she had an idea. She pulled into one of the empty parking spots in front of the café and gazed at the front door with a critical eye. *What do customers see when they look at my café?*

Specifically, she thought of Richard Palmas. What did a man like that see in this place?

Why did Richard think a tourist would want to stop here and come inside?

The café was located in an old, storefront-style building with large windows but not a single distinctive feature. She examined the front door and wondered why she hadn't noticed how desperately it needed to be painted.

"This is awful," she mumbled to herself as she got out of the car and took in the first impression. Stepping inside the café and looking around, Genevieve became aware of how dark it was. The kitchen was nice and bright. She had seen to that by having new, brighter lightbulbs installed in the kitchen the first day she tried to cook in there. But the dining area still had a drab and dingy hue. Especially on a rainy day like today.

"We need some light in here," Genevieve said, joining Leah at the register. "Light and color. And maybe an awning over the front door to allow customers a chance to step out of the rain. I had no idea how little changing the tables and chairs did to improve this place. All my attention has been in the kitchen and on the menu."

"And on the bookkeeping and bills," Leah added.

"There has to be something we can do that won't cost a lot."

"Like what?"

"I don't know. Pads for the chairs would be a good start. And brighter lightbulbs." Genevieve tilted her head up to examine the overhead lighting fixtures. "Look at this ceiling. It's dirty. Did you ever notice that before?"

"No, and neither has anyone else. This is a very old building." Leah returned to the kitchen. "I grew up here, remember? What you've done in two months is a vast improvement. If you start looking for the negative, you'll always find it, Gena. We have to focus on the positive."

Genevieve excused herself and went into the tiny restroom

to wash her hands. She examined her reflection in the mirror. Dozens of fine lines gathered around her eyes and across her forehead, giving her a permanently worried look. She always had considered herself to be an average-looking woman. Pretty sometimes, when she took a little extra care, but certainly not beautiful. Her eyes were a clear, gray color and deeply set above high cheekbones. She thought her mouth was too wide and her lips too thick. When she complained once, Steven immediately disagreed. He said she had "beckoning lips," and then he raved about how great a kisser she was.

I wonder what Richard Palmas saw when he looked at me?

Genevieve immediately rebuked herself. *Where did that come from? Don't open that door, Gena. You know better.*

Turning on the water, she washed her hands thoroughly and hoped she had cleansed her thoughts as well. *Steven thinks I'm attractive. That's what matters. Not a stranger's opinion.*

Genevieve returned to the kitchen and asked Leah, "Do you have any breakfast orders you need me to start on right away?"

"Not yet. Kenton and Collin are just having coffee and bagels at table seven. It's been real slow this morning."

Genevieve pulled on a clean apron. "I hope I didn't sound like I was worried or complaining a little while ago. I want this place to be something special, you know? I had higher hopes than we've accomplished these first two months."

"It'll come together," Leah said gently. "Two months isn't

very long. Especially when you have such high expectations."

Genevieve knew Leah was right. She did have high
expectations. She always had lived on a ladder of ascending
expectations, but sometimes her hopes weren't realistic.

As Genevieve pulled some eggs from the refrigerator,
she thought about the way she had spent her life dreaming
of an illusive happiness floating just outside her grasp. It
was the same happiness she expected when they had
moved to Glenbrooke. The same happiness she had once
supposed children would bring to their marriage. The same
happiness she believed would flood her life when, as an
idealistic nineteen-year-old, she had married Steven and
moved to the United States.

Genevieve suddenly realized that nothing in her life had
gone the way she had imagined it would. Standing in the
middle of the kitchen of her less than dream-come-true café,
she felt a sense of panic rising.

Leah looked up from the sink where she was rinsing off
a head of lettuce. "Are you okay?"

Genevieve turned. "I have to find a way to improve this
place. This café means everything to me."

"It means a lot to me, too," Leah said. "Things will get
better; you'll see. It takes time. Seth and I sure learned that
while we were building our cabin. We thought it would
never be finished, but now that it's done, my restless husband is looking for a new project to dive into."

"You can send him over here anytime you want."

Leah reached for the freshly brewed pot of coffee. "You

know what? That's not a bad idea. I'm sure Seth would be glad to help out. What would you like him to do?"

Genevieve shrugged. "That's the problem. We don't have money for improvements. About the only thing I can afford would be new lightbulbs."

"How many do you think we need?"

Genevieve stepped into the dining room to count the light fixtures and noticed that two men and a woman had just entered. She recognized the older man as the greeter who had so warmly welcomed Genevieve the first time she visited the community church. She hoped he didn't notice her now.

During the months after they had moved to Glenbrooke, Genevieve faithfully attended church with Anna and Mallory because Steven was rarely home on Sundays. When he wasn't flying all over the world, he was scouting out new fishing spots in the area or going to Eugene to buy parts for his restored Triumph sports car. No one asked where he was.

Genevieve was familiar with the routine because she and the girls had gone to church without Steven for years. That was because Steven didn't go to church. Ever.

As Genevieve's catering business grew, she often had to work straight through the weekend. Soon she settled into a pattern of not going to church, too. Anna and Mallory continued to go. Sometimes they even walked to Glenbrooke Community Church.

Ducking back into the kitchen to avoid being noticed, Genevieve told Leah, "I think twelve lightbulbs would do it.

Do you think Seth could bring over your tall ladder to help me replace the lightbulbs after we close this evening?"

"Sure. I'll call him."

Leah returned to the dining room, and a moment later, Genevieve heard her give an enthusiastic hello to the party that had entered. "Teri," Leah cried, "I can't believe you're here! It's so good to see you. You look great! And Gordon." Leah paused before adding in a teasing voice, "Gordon, you look the same."

All of them laughed, and Genevieve thought of what a great asset Leah was to the café and to her life. Leah knew everyone in Glenbrooke, and many of the older customers seemed to show up every morning more for Leah's comforting words than for the coffee. Genevieve reminded herself that her expectation in a suitable partner for the restaurant had been more than met.

"Guess what?" Leah announced breathlessly as she swished into the kitchen. "Gordon and Teri are hoping to move back here. Gordon is interviewing for the position of pastor at church. Isn't that great?"

Genevieve nodded, hoping she appeared enthusiastic about Leah's friends, even though she didn't know them. The truth was, she hadn't even known the church had lost its previous pastor since she hadn't attended for so long.

"Are the cinnamon rolls out of the oven yet?" Leah asked. "I promised Gordon a warm cinnamon roll. And do we have any pineapple? Gordon and Teri live on Maui, and I thought it would be a nice touch to add a pineapple ring to each of their plates."

"Sure, we have pineapple. I might even have a little paper umbrella or two in a drawer."

"Perfect!" Leah placed a comforting hand on Genevieve's shoulder. "I know you're concerned about the café, but try not to be, Gena. You know that Seth and I will both help any way we can. Don't get discouraged. I'm sure you can dream up a little renovation plan for us that won't cost too much."

Leah's words of encouragement did wonders for Genevieve since one of the areas she was good in was planning. Within two days she had eighteen pages of plans for improving the dining area of the Wildflower Café and already had begun to implement some of them.

When she was upgrading the kitchen, she had come up with a single page of plans. Her initial planning efforts for the café were along the lines of signing and filing all necessary business papers, doing an inventory of kitchen equipment, going through her recipes, and getting new menus printed.

Planning the aesthetic dimension of the café was much more fun. It energized Genevieve in the same way planning her elaborate garden in Pasadena had enlivened her for several years.

By Friday, the third morning after Leah had challenged Genevieve to dream up some plans for improvement, Genevieve was filled with hope. She parked behind the Wildflower Café and walked around to the front to view her handiwork from the past few days.

A smile came to her lips.

The flowerboxes she had found in the café's back storage shed worked perfectly. She painted them a bright blue, and the next day, Seth came over and attached them securely in place under the front windows.

This morning the new flowerboxes glistened in the sunlight. White alyssum spilled over the sides while blue and yellow pansies turned their faces toward the welcome sunbeams. Stately daffodils nodded their heads, looking like contented cats preening themselves in the warm window box. Several of the red tulips stretched their necks and appeared ready to yawn themselves open at any minute.

"That's what we needed," Genevieve said proudly. "What a difference."

Nearly every customer had commented on the flowerboxes the day before, when the flowers made their debut. Leah delighted in telling everyone that they were the original flowerboxes Genevieve had found in the back shed and that all the flowers had been donated by long-time Glenbrooke resident, Ida Dane. At Leah's request, Ida had dug up the bulbs and flowers from her extensive garden and had brought several buckets to the café. She had insisted that she be the one to arrange them. Ida's final results had been rewarded with lunch on the house and all of Leah's free publicity.

Genevieve stood another moment, admiring the transformation brought about by the three window flowerboxes. She especially was pleased because it had cost her nothing. Even the blue paint, which she had found on a clearance rack at the hardware store, was free. When Mack at the hardware store heard what Genevieve was using the paint for, he told her she could have it at no charge. Any other supplies she needed for repairs at the Wildflower Café would be discounted. All she had to do was ask for Mack when she came in.

"I've been eating at that café since I was a kid," Mack had told her. "We all were worried that it might close down for good before you bought it. They say that when a small town is about to die, the restaurants and gas stations close up. When you bought the place, I don't mind telling you, quite a few of us had high hopes for Glenbrooke's future."

Genevieve hadn't felt stunned or pressured by his comments the way she had when Richard Palmas made some of the same statements. Instead, Mack's words became a gentle blessing and mandate from Glenbrooke's older residents. Mack made her feel as if she were carrying out a noble mission to revive the café. With such support and encouragement, she was more hopeful than ever that she could get her little business to turn the corner and start showing a profit.

With the flowerboxes taken care of, Genevieve's attention was focused on the front door. She had considered painting it bright blue as well but wasn't sure if that would work. One thought had been to paint all the wooden tables and chairs bright primary colors to give customers the feeling that they were stepping into a field of wildflowers at the height of summer. But then the walls would definitely need to be repainted, and the cost would add up. Even with a discount on the paint, it would be too expensive.

Genevieve wasn't ready to make any decisions on the door or interior yet; she was still in the envisioning stage.

That's the process she had used when she created her garden in Pasadena. For hours she would study garden magazines, cutting out pictures and making notes. Then she would take her notebook of clippings and scribbled thoughts outside and sit on the grass in the open, undeveloped space between her house and the set of duplexes they rented out.

Genevieve would sit for only ten or fifteen minutes at a time, gazing at the pictures in her notebook, then gazing at the various corners and pockets of the yard. She would close her eyes, trying to envision where each gathering of flowers would go. Then she would walk away and think about it while she made dinner or folded laundry. By the time she turned up the first shovelful of dirt, she had "lived" with the proposed idea long enough to have considered every pro and con and worked through possible problems. The results in the garden were spectacular.

Genevieve wanted those kinds of results now for the Wildflower Café. Her major obstacles were time and money. With her garden she had spent years working on it at her leisure. Money hadn't been a problem then. Money wouldn't be a problem now if she were working on the garden at their home. She had a substantial budget to work with at home.

The café was another story because it was on a different budget. Funds for the restaurant came from a separate bank account. Steven's greatest concern when Genevieve wanted to buy the café was that it would drain their personal savings and put them in financial difficulties. They had agreed to keep the café finances separate, with Genevieve agreeing not to dip into their family funds to cover the café's expenses. If she needed more money for the restaurant, she would take out a loan at the bank. If she couldn't make the loan payments, she would sell the café or declare bankruptcy. Clear and simple.

Genevieve shook away the reoccurring thought that she was slowly heading for bankruptcy. But for now the flowerboxes were enough of a day brightener to prompt her to enter the café smiling. Her grin broadened when she heard the lilting melody of the tiny wind chimes she had hung over the door. The chimes had also been in the café's storage shed out back. They were too small and too rusted to be used out front where someone would notice them. But when Seth had climbed up on the tall ladder to change the lightbulbs last night, it occurred to Genevieve they could hang the wind chimes on a peg high enough above the door that they wouldn't be noticed but they would be ruffled by the air every time the door opened.

The sound was subtle and pleasing. So was the improved lighting. Although, the sun's bold appearance today was probably the real reason for the bright and cheerful atmosphere inside the café.

Genevieve glanced around at the tables. Yes, something definitely needed to be done with the tables and chairs. But the good news was more people were in the café than usual, and it wasn't quite eight o'clock yet. She counted only three empty tables. That was a new record.

"Good morning," Genevieve greeted one of the diners by the window.

"G'day," he replied. "Glorious day, isn't it?"

She thought his accent was most likely Australian and that she had seen him in the café before, but she wasn't sure if she knew him.

"Yes, it is a beautiful day." Genevieve hurried back into the kitchen where Leah was moving around like a frenzied cottontail rabbit.

"I'm so glad you're here! It's been busy for an hour. What happened? Did all the groundhogs in Glenbrooke decide to come out the same morning just for the phenomenon of see-ing their own shadows?"

Genevieve laughed. "I think the flowerboxes lured them here." She tied on her apron and noticed that Leah was wear-ing a khaki skirt with a slit in the back rather than her usual jeans and T-shirt. The style wasn't particularly flattering for Leah's short, thick legs, but she looked fresh and crisp with her white shirtsleeves rolled up. The baseball cap was gone this morning as well. Instead, Leah wore a row of tiny, glit-tering clips to keep back her hair.

"You certainly look fresh today," Genevieve said. "Here, let me flip those pancakes for you. I can take over if you need to serve some of these."

"Thanks. We need two more orders of pancakes, one ham and cheese omelet with an English muffin, lightly toasted, and a scrambled with well-done hash browns and sourdough toast. Did you get all that?"

"Yes, I think so."

Leah left with three plates in her hands and called out over her shoulder, "I'll start writing down the orders."

Up until now, they had rarely been busy enough for Leah to take notes, plus many of the customers ordered the same thing everyday. Even they knew how costly paper was and told her to save the expense. Besides, Genevieve had a great memory and didn't usually need Leah to write out the orders for her.

Genevieve worked quickly. The morning rush calmed down around nine-thirty as usual, and Genevieve prepared the soup of the day in a large pot. The soup of the day and the dessert of the day came from her favorite recipes. Her carrot cake was by far the favorite dessert of the day. The favorite soup of the day came from a Glenbrooke resident and appeared on the menu as Jessica's Broccoli Cheese Soup. It was requested as often as the clam chowder. Leah was the one who had suggested that Genevieve feature special recipes for the soups and desserts of the day.

As Genevieve loaded the industrial dishwasher, she thought about showing her notebook of café ideas and pictures to Leah. It felt like a bold step because she usually kept things to herself. She had spent most of her life making all the necessary decisions on her own. When Steven was home, he usually had some input, but Genevieve was the one who considered all the options and suggested the final course of action on everything from buying a new washing machine to hanging a mirror instead of a picture over the living room fireplace.

Plus she had been telling herself for a long time she didn't need anyone. Ever since she had closed up her heart for a season of silent winter in her soul, Genevieve's circle of relationships had grown smaller and smaller. She didn't want anyone knocking on her heart's door or trying to pull the boards off the windows. She could take care of herself.

But right now, in this situation, it felt different to open herself up to Leah. Leah felt like a partner and had good insights. This was business, after all, not personal. It was about consulting someone else to do everything possible to make the café succeed. And in a very limited way, Genevieve felt she could trust Leah. Yes, Leah's opinions on the proposed changes to the café would be helpful.

Genevieve waited until later that day when only two people were in the café. Leah was seated on a stool in the kitchen, eating pasta salad out of a coffee cup.

"Leah," Genevieve forced herself to say, "may I show you something?"

Chapter Three

eah didn't say a word as Genevieve went through the long lists and showed Leah the pictures she had cut from various magazines. When they reached the last page, Genevieve cast a shy glance at Leah. "Well, what do you think?"

"I think you're a genius." Leah's apple-round cheeks turned pink as she spoke. "All of these ideas are really good. I love the one about designing a separate meeting room in the corner that's partially closed off."

"Do you think that would work? I've been in restaurants before that have quiet spaces like that. I thought it might draw in people for meetings or to have a semiprivate place to celebrate a birthday."

Leah's eyes lit up. "That would definitely attract a younger crowd. Do you remember the other day when Paul was here from church? He was trying to have a meeting with Gordon and Teri, but it was so noisy for them at the middle table that they asked to be moved to the corner table as soon as it opened up."

"That's where I was thinking the semiprivate room should be set up."

"I also like your idea of finding ways to get more children and families to come to the café," Leah said. "You know how much that would change this place? Instead of just being a place to eat, the Wildflower Café would become a gathering place for friends."

Genevieve loved the sound of Leah's words. *A gathering place for friends.* A rush of hope spilled into her spirit. Something inside her said, *Yes, that's what has been missing. You need to provide a gathering place for friends.*

For a moment, Genevieve felt as if a stream of sunlight had burst into her heart. The thought came that she should open her heart's windows, hang a welcome sign over her heart's front door, and invite all her friends to gather there.

Where did that thought come from? We're talking about the café not my life. Genevieve quickly pulled back her feelings. Her heart wasn't open for visitors of any kind. But the café would be. It would take on a new image and draw new customers, and that would provide the necessary revenue to stay open.

"All we need now are some more creative donations like Ida's flowers," Genevieve said, returning to the practical aspects of the moment.

Leah hopped down from the stool and headed for the

dining area to check on the last two customers. "I have a feeling the Lord will provide."

Genevieve couldn't help but wonder if Leah already was thinking of ways to use her connections around town to help the Lord provide. When Genevieve first had moved to Glenbrooke, she had heard from her friend Alissa that Leah was called "the Glenbrooke Zorro" because for years she quietly gave to people who were in need. As a matter of fact, because of Leah's generosity a number of new utensils were being used in the café's kitchen. Leah had claimed they were wedding gift duplicates and that, by donating them to the Wildflower kitchen, she could use them everyday, whereas at home they would sit in a drawer.

"We should check the storage shed again," Leah suggested. "We might find a few more treasures in all that stuff."

Genevieve decided she would have a look as soon as she finished unloading the dishwasher, which was her final task for the day. Before she stacked the last plate, her two daughters, Mallory and Anna, entered the café.

"I thought you two were going home after school," Genevieve said.

"You told us we could come here any time we wanted," Mallory sputtered. At ten years old, she was the one who always came up with the quickest responses. Anna was more shy and reserved, like Genevieve.

"Of course you can come here. Any time. I love having you with me. I'm almost finished so we can all go home in a few minutes."

"Don't you have anything more to do here?" Mallory's

cocoa brown eyes took on the same look Steven's eyes had whenever he couldn't find his favorite pair of reading glasses.

"Not really," Genevieve said.

"You don't have anything else to paint?" Anna asked.

"No."

"Because we can help," Anna said. "If you want us to. I mean, with painting or something fun like that."

Genevieve's pulse beat a little faster. Aside from asking to lick the bowl after she made brownies for catering events, this was the first time her serious middle daughter had expressed interest in being involved in what Genevieve did.

"You know what?" Genevieve smiled at Anna. "I'm glad you asked. I should have suggested you paint the flower-boxes the other night. You love that sort of thing. The key to the shed is on the hook by the back door. You're welcome to go out there and see what you can find. Anything that looks worth saving or painting is available to you. Your creative touches will help make the café special."

"Me, too?" Mallory asked.

Genevieve caught a look of older sister disapproval on Anna's face. "No, I have another project for you in here," Genevieve told Mallory.

"What? Are you making cookies?"

"Yes. Cookies are the dessert of the day for tomorrow. You can help me with them now, and that will save me some time in the morning."

"Can I wear an apron?" Mallory reached for one of the aprons on the hook by the sink.

"Of course. Here, let me tie that for you."

An hour and a half later, Genevieve and the girls climbed into the van. They each had a warm, white chocolate chip macadamia nut cookie. An old rusted bicycle was crammed in the van's back along with three old, wooden picture frames and a box of soiled linens. Anna also had found a chair with an unusual, thin metal frame. The chair didn't fit in the van along with the bike so they left it under a tree beside the storage shed.

"Can I paint the frames any way I want?" Anna asked.

"Yes, of course."

"Do you promise you'll use them at the café no matter how I decorate them?"

"Yes, I promise." Genevieve had no problem making such a promise because Anna was artistic. She first showed her ability when she was around eight. But it wasn't through coloring or drawing; it was when she wrapped Christmas gifts. She had a knack for selecting unlikely materials and putting them together to make beautiful packages.

Genevieve decided that turning the frames over to Anna without giving her direction would be a good thing for Anna. It would be a good thing for their mother-daughter relationship. No matter how the frames turned out, Genevieve could find a use for them and a way to praise Anna.

Before Anna went to bed that night, she presented Genevieve with her first finished frame. Anna had painted the frame white with tiny blue and yellow flowers weaving up the sides. The look was fresh and appealing. Across the bottom she had written with flowing letters: "Consider the lilies of the field."

"It's very pretty," Genevieve said. "Where did you find the little quote at the bottom?"

"From the Bible. Matthew 6. I tried to find other Bible verses on flowers, but there weren't very many. I'll paint the other two frames tomorrow because I want to finish my postcards for literature now. They aren't due until next week, but I don't want to have any homework over the weekend."

"Postcards?"

"We had to take our favorite lines from the short stories we've been reading and make postcards."

"That sounds like a creative way to do a book report," Genevieve said. "I'd like to see what you came up with."

"I've finished two." Anna brushed her fine, blond hair off her forehead. She shyly pulled two postcards from her backpack and showed them to Genevieve.

The first one had a bright yellow border around it with a simple blue bottle in the right corner. In the center was printed, "I could have sat down on the spot and cried heartily, if I had not learned the wisdom of bottling up one's tears for leisure moments."

Genevieve chuckled. "Who wrote that?"

"Louisa May Alcott. See? It says so on the back. And this other one is also hers."

Genevieve read the second postcard, which was ornately decorated with Victorian-style Valentine hearts. "These faulty hearts of ours cannot turn perfect in a night; but need frost and fire, wind and rain, to ripen and make them ready for the great harvest-home."

"You have a wonderful talent, Anna. These are darling postcards."

Anna seemed to soak up Genevieve's praise. She flitted over to the refrigerator as graceful as a butterfly. Pouring herself a glass of orange juice, she said, "Mom, do you save up all your tears?"

"Save up my tears? Oh, you mean like in your quote?"

Anna nodded. "Do you ever save up your tears for a leisure moment?"

"I don't think so."

"I never see you cry." Anna tilted her head. "At least I don't remember seeing you cry for a really long time."

Genevieve shrugged. "I suppose I don't have much to cry about. That's a good thing, isn't it?"

Anna didn't respond. Genevieve picked up a sponge and automatically wiped off the kitchen counters.

"Mom?" Anna lowered herself to a kitchen stool, as if preparing for a long answer. "Do you love Dad?"

"Of course I love him," Genevieve said quickly. "We've been married for twenty-six years. Why do you ask such a question?"

Anna's tenderness and intense perception seemed to increase the older she became. Genevieve wondered if Anna had discerned the aloofness that had been growing between Genevieve and Steven over the last few years.

"I just wondered." Anna stayed put, as Genevieve cleaned around her. "Mom, would you and Dad ever divorce?"

"No, we're committed to each other."

"Do you know Tanya in my class?"

"I don't think so."

"She's moving next week because her parents are divorcing. She and her mom are going to live in Idaho with her aunt. Tanya doesn't like Idaho. She doesn't like her aunt or her cousins, either."

"Are you afraid that's what might happen to you someday?" Genevieve tried to make her voice sound sure and comforting.

"I just think that divorce happens to people you don't expect it to happen to."

"That's true." Genevieve tossed the sponge into the sink and gave Anna what she hoped was an encouraging smile. "I don't think that will ever happen with your father and me."

"Are you sure?"

Genevieve ignored the uncertain feelings that were dashing about inside her. "Yes, I'm sure."

"Even if Dad decided to live with another woman the way Tanya's dad did?"

Genevieve's pulse pounded in her ears. "Anna, I don't know what happened with Tanya and her family, but that's her family, not ours. Your father and I have been through a lot over the years, and we're still together. We plan to stay together for the rest of our lives."

"That's what I hoped you would say." Anna finished the last of her orange juice. "I don't want to move again, and I really don't ever want to have to decide between living with you or Dad. I want us always to be together."

"That's what we want, too."

After Anna went to bed, Genevieve lowered herself into her mother's antique rocking chair by the window. The shades were up, and the world beyond her cozy corner was illuminated with moonlight, the blessing of a clear night. No streetlights were near the backyard to compete with the shimmering moon. She loved the solitude that surrounded their Glenbrooke home.

With a sigh, Genevieve thought about Anna's questions. She wondered where Steven was right now. Was he flying over the Pacific Ocean? Or was he about to land a plane on a runway somewhere across the world where the sun had not yet set?

He's been a wonderful father to the girls. And he loves me. I know he loves me. The problem with our marriage is me. I'm the one who has grown cold.

An image of her mother came to mind. Most evenings while Genevieve was growing up, her mother sat in this same rocking chair with her glasses balanced on the bridge of her nose. She was always working on something. If she wasn't knitting a cap for the little shop in Zurich where she sold her handmade wares, she was crocheting a baby blanket. Genevieve still had the baby blankets her mother had made for each of Genevieve's daughters. Those three blankets and a blue-and-red ski sweater from when Genevieve was eight years old were the only bits of her mother's handiwork she still had.

When Genevieve's parents had passed away, her relationship with both of them was strong and close, even though it hadn't always been that way. Her father was nearly fifty when she was born, and her mother was forty-two. Genevieve was their only child, and she had grown up hearing often that she was "the nicest surprise" they ever had.

It occurred to Genevieve that she had never doubted her parent's love and admiration for her even though the words "I love you" were rarely spoken. She didn't remember ever asking her parents if they were considering a divorce even though their marriage never displayed much evidence that they loved each other. They were simply together all the time. Their demeanor was courteous, and their conversations were brief and cordial.

Genevieve stared out the window at the moonlight on the lawn. The backyard needed so much work. The rain had caused the weeds to sprout with zeal. Clearly no one had put much time into the backyard for years before Steven and Genevieve had moved in. When they bought the house, she thought she would enjoy creating a special garden, as she had in Pasadena. But then the catering business became too demanding, and she found it easier to ignore the massive amount of work the yard needed.

She thought about her father and how he had praised her Pasadena garden the two times he had visited the family in California. The garden was in its earliest stages when he had plucked a tall Shasta daisy and twirled it between his long fingers. If he had been wearing a suit at that moment, Genevieve was certain he would have tucked the daisy into his lapel buttonhole and worn it all day.

In most of her memories of him, Genevieve's father wore

a dark suit. He had worked for a bank in Zurich for almost forty years. He spoke three languages fluently and insisted that English be spoken in the home.

She remembered the way her papa walked her to school every morning, drilling her on English verbs as her short legs hurried to keep up with his vigorous stride. He would deposit her at the front gate of her school with a courteous half-bow and a phrase in German that loosely translated meant, "Make something of your life that will shine brightly." Then, without looking back, he would turn on his heels to catch the tram to the downtown financial district.

Genevieve smiled to herself when she thought of how her mother's life was more of a gentle glow than a "bright shine." She was an at-home mom whose mission in life, it seemed, was to keep their small city apartment extra clean, as if they were expecting important company at any minute. Yet they almost never entertained.

It was a good life. A simple one.

The memories of her quiet childhood were partially what had drawn Genevieve to Glenbrooke. She had wanted a slower pace than the life she had in southern California. Somehow she had convinced herself long ago that her marriage wouldn't be solid until she and her husband spent evenings together in their rocking chairs, with Steven reading the paper and Genevieve busy with handiwork in her lap.

The image caused Genevieve to shake her head. *Where did I come up with that? I don't even like to knit.*

It occurred to Genevieve that in one way she was following her parents' example in her own marriage. She was courteous and satisfied with being cordial and brief with her husband while curtailing any outward expression of her love for him. Perhaps Anna had to ask if Genevieve loved Steven because her actions didn't make it obvious.

Is that so unusual? Genevieve asked herself. *Don't all couples our age settle into such a routine? What's wrong with living in a state of courteous companionship?*

Genevieve thought about how she had come to be in this "cordial" season of their marriage. She knew the exact moment when it began. It was the day after her forty-third birthday, a cloudy afternoon almost three years ago. Steven had met her in the garden of their Pasadena home with his captain's hat in his hand. He lowered his head and made a solemn apology to her in front of the snapdragons.

Genevieve didn't cry. She didn't tell him what she really thought. Instead, she stopped weeding and took off her gardening gloves. In a calm, cordial tone she stated, "It's okay. I understand, Steven. The stock market is risky. We both knew that. It may turn around in the next few weeks."

However, their investments didn't turn around that week or any week after that. More than half of the inheritance Genevieve had received from her parents' estate had been lost on a high risk stock that Steven had felt sure was going to triple. All her father's hard-earned money was gone, just like that.

And she felt horribly guilty.

A long-repressed tear slipped out and trailed down Genevieve's cheek as she stared out the window at the dark shadows stretching across the lawn. *I know it wasn't Steven's fault. We both agreed on where the money should be invested. It's not as if it was all lost. We still had enough to buy the café.*

Wrapping her arms around herself, Genevieve rocked and wished Steven were there to hold her. He never was home when she needed him most. Like the night she had received the phone call that her mother had passed away. Or the afternoon she went into labor with Mallory, three weeks before the due date.

Steven has simply not been there for me.

A stream of tears came, blurring her vision of the world beyond the familiar rocking chair. With her tears came a rush of criticism toward herself for being so overwhelmed. *Snap out of it, Genevieve! You have no reason to feel so sorry for yourself. It's not as if Steven is moving in with another woman and leaving you forever. He has been a good father. He has provided for you and your daughters in a generous way over the years. Your inheritance money wasn't something you needed to survive.*

The tears didn't respond to her logic. The hurt was very real to her heart. With the moonlight as her only witness, Genevieve rocked in her mother's chair and cried out all the bottled-up tears she had saved, without realizing it, for such a leisure moment.

Chapter Four

The only conclusion Genevieve came to after her night of swimming in her tears by moonlight was that the Wildflower Café was now the embodiment of all her dreams and expectations. It was her one chance to make good on what had remained of the inheritance money, a chance to "make something of her life that will shine brightly."

Genevieve spent the next few days focusing on her redecorating efforts. She decided to put more work into fixing up the front of the Wildflower while the weather was nice.

Steven called a few days before he came home, and Anna answered the phone. She bubbled over with descriptions for her father about her involvement in sprucing up the café. She described the four wooden frames she had salvaged from the shed and how they were all freshly painted, decorated, and ready for pictures worthy of their charm.

Then she told him about how she had spent the weekend cleaning up the old bicycle, painting the fenders deep red and artistically positioning it in front of the café.

"Seth wired the bike to the wall," Anna told him. "Not because we're afraid that anyone would want to steal it. It's because it's such a relic. Seth said the bike is being held together with fresh paint on top of the rust and the wire we used to connect it to the wall."

Genevieve stopped in the middle of helping Mallory with a math problem and listened to the delight in her middle daughter's voice. Anna was telling her father customers' comments about the café's front. Then she asked a favor that Genevieve knew Steven would be happy to fulfill.

"Dad, when you get home Thursday, will you pick me up after school and come see the front of the café with me?"

The spring rains returned on Thursday, and so did Steven.

He picked up Anna after school. Genevieve joined them in front of the café and held a wide umbrella so Steven could conduct his own shower of praise on Anna.

Genevieve couldn't hide her pride and enthusiasm for her daughter and for the café. The inside still needed a lot of attention, but the entrance was 1000 percent more appealing than it had been.

"I heard some people say they think it looks like a European café now," Anna said. "Is that what you think, Dad?"

Steven's arm encompassed Anna's shoulders. He was out

of his pilot's uniform and wearing jeans and his favorite shirt, a long-sleeved, oatmeal-colored knit shirt Genevieve had ordered for him from a catalog at Christmas. It made him look cuddly and tender, which was how Anna was responding to him now.

"Definitely." Steven drew Anna close. "European all the way. Nice work, Anna."

"Thanks, Dad."

From the way Anna was beaming, Genevieve could tell his simple words of praise sunk deeper into Anna's heart than the days of praise Genevieve had given her. Once again she felt like the one who did all the work, only to watch Steven step in at the time of harvest and scoop up the best of the crop.

"I think when I grow up I want to be an exterior decorator, if there is such a thing," Anna said. "I want to help people make the outside of their homes beautiful."

Genevieve watched Steven smile at Anna. They were the romantics in the family. The two artistic spirits who conversed in their own special language. This wasn't the first time Genevieve had felt like an outsider when Steven and Anna were having a meeting of the minds.

"Are either of you interested in some soup?" Genevieve asked.

Steven and Anna both turned and looked at her as if they couldn't imagine anyone thinking of her stomach at a time like this. They were admiring art. Such a moment shouldn't be rushed.

"I'm going inside," Genevieve said quietly. She handed

the umbrella to Steven and made her way through the café to the kitchen, feeling chilled in her cotton sweater and jeans skirt. "It would be so nice to have a fireplace in here," she muttered to herself.

"Did you say something?" Leah stood in the middle of the kitchen holding a large, long box.

"I was just saying that a fireplace in here would sure be nice."

"Wow! That's really expanding your vision," Leah said. "I don't know if we can get a fireplace in here, but look at what Mack just brought over from the hardware store. I traded him for this."

Leah slit open the end of the box. "Mack was in here the other day and said he had been getting requests for flower-boxes ever since you put up yours. He doesn't have any ready-made ones and most people don't want to make theirs. I told him that Seth and I would make twenty flower-boxes from the scrap lumber left over from our cabin if we could trade them for an awning."

"An awning?"

Leah pulled the long, royal blue canvas awning from the box. "For the front door. Didn't you say you wanted an awning to cover the front?"

"Yes, but Leah you didn't have to do this."

"I know. I wanted to. It matches the flowerboxes. With the bicycle and flowers out front, this awning is going to make the Wildflower Café the best looking storefront on Main Street. Oh, and Mack said he would sand the door for you if you decide you want to paint it. But he agreed with me when I said I think it looks good the way it is, especially with the original, beveled glass at the top and the original brass handle. It's classic Glenbrooke."

"Leah, this is so kind of you." Genevieve felt the blue canvas. "Thank you."

"You're welcome. I need to get that turkey sandwich to table two." Leah slipped out with the serving plate in her hand just as Steven and Anna entered the kitchen. Over her shoulder Leah said, "Don't forget to ask Steven what he thinks about our idea of selling the tables."

"What idea is that?" Steven headed for the refrigerator and pulled out the cheesecake, counting the precut slices. "Mind if I have one? It looks like three slices are left."

"Sure, help yourself. Did you see the strawberries? They should be in a bowl behind the ham."

"Found it." Steven prepared the afternoon dessert while Genevieve served up the last portion of vegetable lasagna.

Leah swished in, picked up the lasagna and a plate with a Caesar salad and returned to the dining room.

The good thing about the kitchen being blocked off from the customers was that no one could see her husband perched on the counter eating strawberry cheesecake or her daughter using the telephone on the back wall.

"What was the idea about the tables?" Steven asked again.

"Shelly and Jonathan out at Camp Heather Brook want to buy all the tables and chairs from the café and use them at the camp. They told us this morning and asked if we could deliver them before Shelly's May Day event in two weeks."

Steven looked confused. "Why would you sell the tables?"

"They're too big. Most of our diners are couples or groups of four. The tables are so large people have to raise their voices to have conversations. The other problem is that the chairs are uncomfortable."

Steven nodded and licked the back of his fork. "I noticed that."

Genevieve looked at her husband. "Did you say anything about it to me before?"

"No. I thought it would be pointless since you had just bought them."

"I think that's what everybody thought. I didn't make a good choice on the tables and chairs. Selling them to Shelly and Jonathan would give me enough money to start over."

"Are you going to install booths like they had here before?" Steven asked.

"No, I was thinking of smaller tables. Leah suggested a mixture of different sizes, shapes, and colors. She saw several at the antique store, but I'm not convinced that all that color and contrast would work."

"I liked the booths by the windows," Steven said. "They were comfortable and more private."

"Yes, but remember all the torn places on the vinyl seats and how they had repaired them with duct tape?"

Steven nodded and placed his plate and fork in the sink. "Except for that, I liked the booths. But they were old. Maybe something manufactured during this millennium would stand the wear and tear better." He came over to where Genevieve was cleaning the stove and wrapped his arms around her waist. "How about if you and I go to the coast this weekend?"

"This weekend?" Genevieve asked.

"Yeah, this weekend. How about it?"

"We could get away on Sunday afternoon," Genevieve said. "The girls have been wanting to go back to the tide pools ever since we were there last August."

"I meant just the two of us. For the whole weekend." Steven kissed Genevieve's neck.

She was about to say she couldn't leave the café, but Leah entered and said, "Okay, you two, I saw that. No kissing the cook when she's working."

Steven pressed a deliberate kiss on Genevieve's cheek. "I'll make all the arrangements. We can leave tomorrow as soon as you close up shop. I have to fly out on Monday."

"Monday?" Genevieve turned and looked at Steven. "You just got back. Why so soon?"

"Route changes. On Monday I fly to Denver for a meeting."

"How can you fly again so soon? Aren't you supposed to have a longer layover? That doesn't seem right. Are you sure you have to go?"

Genevieve didn't care if her daughter on the phone or Leah, who was loading the dishwasher, heard her less than cordial response to Steven's announcement.

"I have to be there for the meeting," he said. "And I won't be the pilot on the flight to Hong Kong. I'm one of a dozen pilots who are being cross trained for a new route. I'll be there for three days, and then I return and connect with my usual route from Singapore."

The details only confused Genevieve.

Steven kissed her again. "I told Mallory I'd pick her up after soccer practice. Think about this weekend and tell me when you get home." Turning to Anna, he said, "Are you ready to go, Sunshine?"

The two of them were about to leave when Leah closed up the dishwasher and asked Steven, "So what do you think about our idea to sell the tables and chairs?"

"Whatever you want to do is fine with me."

Genevieve clenched her teeth. For years Steven had given her that answer to a wide variety of her questions. It didn't matter if her question was, "What do you want to name our daughter?" or "Which restaurant would you like to go to?" Steven responded with the same line.

"It's always up to me," Genevieve muttered.

Leah leaned against the counter. "I wish my hubby were as easygoing as yours. Seth is more opinionated than I am when it comes to details. Sometimes I wish he would just leave the decision up to me so I didn't have to filter everything through all his preferences."

Genevieve pressed her lips together and vigorously scrubbed around the burner on the stove. She knew Leah had a point. She should consider Steven's trust in her decisions an indication of his confidence in her.

"Tell Shelly we'll sell the tables," Genevieve said suddenly to Leah. "Tell her we can deliver them sometime next week."

"How about next Wednesday?" Leah asked. "Seth said he could borrow one of the PDS trucks from work and take all the tables to Camp Heather Brook in one trip."

Genevieve nodded. Leah's being married to a man who worked for a delivery service was a nice advantage. "That would be great. Tell Seth I'll be happy to pay him for the gas and his time."

"That's not a problem," Leah said. "We can work something out."

"Now we need to get some new tables."

"Have you had a look at Lauren's antique shop? You could stop by there on your way home."

"Good idea. Oh, and, Leah, I have one more situation to figure out. Steven wants to go to the coast this weekend, but—"

Leah jumped in. "Sounds like a great idea. Have fun."

"No, we're not going," Genevieve said. "What it made me think of is that for future weekends, when either one of us needs a Saturday off, we should interview those women you told me about. I'm hoping that we'll see business pick up soon. When we do, we'll need to hire someone part time to fill in for us."

"Finding someone to work here isn't a problem," Leah said. "I can get a high school girl to come in Saturday and train her. It's not that busy. I could run the whole café by myself on Saturday if I needed to. You should go. Really, Gena. As your friend, I'm telling you, you need to get out of here for a few days. It will freshen up your perspective on life."

"I don't think this would be a good time to get away."

"If you're thinking you shouldn't go because of the café, I'm sure I can handle things. You really should take advantage of the time since Steven is home. Did I hear that he's flying out again Monday?"

Genevieve nodded.

"You should go," Leah said firmly.

Genevieve hadn't expected such a strong response from Leah. But Genevieve felt certain that if she tried to come up with a reason she shouldn't go to the coast with Steven, Leah would come up with a stronger reason for her to go.

"Well," Genevieve said thoughtfully, "maybe we could leave Saturday right after lunch."

Leah shook her head. "Why? You should go Friday. When was the last time you and Steven had time together like this?"

Genevieve thought hard and couldn't remember.

"Do you need some recommendations for places to stay?" Leah asked.

"I don't think so. Steven said he would make all the arrangements."

Leah flipped her short blond hair behind her ear. "Your husband is a honey."

Genevieve thought her "honey's" surprising her with the invitation to go away for the weekend sure blew a hole in her theory that he didn't care about details or that if anything was going to get done, she was the one who would have to do it.

"I'll think about it," Genevieve said.

"Well, just in case you decide to go, what is the dessert of the day for Saturday?"

"It's carrot cake."

"Why don't we make the cake now, just in case you go? It's becoming one of the favorites around here. If Kenton knows that's what we're serving Saturday, he'll be in here for sure."

"I suppose we could do that." Genevieve checked the cupboard to make sure they had enough cans of one of the main ingredients: strained baby food carrots. "I hope you never told Kenton the secret ingredient is baby food. Men have a hard time eating this cake after they find out I didn't puree all the carrots by hand."

Leah laughed. "Don't worry. Your secret ingredient is safe with me." She paused and added, "Any secret you want to share is safe with me."

Genevieve felt a twinge of uncomfortableness. She didn't know if Leah was hinting at something or merely being friendly. Genevieve wasn't looking for anyone with whom she could share secrets or open up.

Leah plugged in the mixer and adjusted the mixing bowl. "Tell me again where you got this recipe. Wasn't it from a friend in Pasadena?"

"Yes, Carolyn was a good friend. She was the woman who invited me to go to a women's Bible study with her six years ago."

"And that was the first time you had ever gone to church," Leah added. "You told me before that at that Bible study you gave your life to Christ, right?"

"That's right." Genevieve didn't add any other information and hoped that Leah would drop the subject.

But Leah seemed to be on a particularly determined streak today. "You told me once that Steven has never gone to church with you. Has he ever shown any interest in spiritual matters?"

Now Genevieve felt as if her headstrong copartner was going too far. Leah couldn't possibly understand how difficult this conversation was for her. "I'm sure Steven is just as interested in spiritual matters as the next person. He just doesn't choose to go to church."

"Well, I hope he'll come sometime and hear our new pastor. You've met Gordon and his wife, Teri. They've been in here before. Remember? They're the ones who are moving to Glenbrooke from Maui. Trust me, Gordo isn't like any other pastor you've ever heard. I think you'll like him a lot. Why don't you guys come with us this Sunday and then have lunch at our house afterwards?"

"We might go to the coast this weekend, remember?"

"Oh, of course."

Genevieve felt relieved that she had a legitimate reason for being gone Sunday.

"Maybe next weekend," Leah said.

"Maybe." Genevieve turned to the mixing bowl into which she had dumped the carrot cake ingredients.

Steven's unresponsiveness over the years when Genevieve had asked him to go to church was such a deeply buried hurt that she felt irritated with Leah for bringing it up. It wasn't as if Genevieve hadn't faithfully prayed for her husband. She had for years. She had tried everything from bribing him with Sunday morning waffles and strawberries before the service to shaming him, saying he was a poor example to their daughters.

None of her tactics had changed anything. Steven never had gone to church with her. He hadn't hindered or discouraged her or the girls, but he simply had chosen not to join them.

Genevieve watched the ingredients in the mixer as they smushed together. She felt as if her insides were doing the same thing.

Chapter Five

$\mathcal{F}$riday afternoon, Genevieve left the café with plenty of apprehension about being gone all weekend. She reminded Leah four times that she would have her cell phone turned on and that Leah should call about any problem.

Genevieve then drove the girls to their friends' homes where they were staying. When she returned home, she found Steven loading her suitcase into the small trunk of his Triumph.

"The newspaper said the weather should clear up tomorrow on the coast," Steven said. "I thought we would take this car in case we want to do some touring with the top down."

Genevieve nodded. She still wasn't sure why she had agreed to do this. She didn't think it was a direct result of Leah's prompting but rather a mix of reasons. She figured

Anna would feel more secure, knowing her parents were going off together for the weekend. And Genevieve hoped the time away would give her some fresh insights into the café. Spending time alone with Steven wasn't at the top of her list.

They drove in the rain for the better part of an hour with the heater on high and their conversation on low. Steven's car was much noisier than the van, so it wasn't unusual for them to travel in comfortable silence.

Every now and then, Steven commented on the gorgeous Northwest scenery along the two-lane road they were taking to the coast. In the dripping twilight, the towering trees that lined the road did look, as Steven suggested, like friendly giants guarding the forest.

Somewhere between the enchanting cedars and the steady hum of the car's motor, Genevieve told herself to relax and enjoy this weekend. For too long her life had been consumed with planning and doing and fretting. Her weary mind and fragile spirit needed a rest.

Steven turned off the highway and drove down a long, paved driveway. The windshield wipers swished at top speed, smearing the view of the resort's entrance.

"Good evening," a uniformed valet greeted Genevieve as he opened her door under the wide portico. "Welcome to the New Brighton Lodge. Will you be staying with us this evening?"

"Yes," Genevieve answered, getting out of the car.

"The registration desk is through the lobby and to your left."

Genevieve waited for Steven to tip the valet, and the two of them entered together. One of the perks of Steven's job in the travel industry was the great discounts available for resorts, such as the New Brighton Lodge. The unfortunate truth was that they rarely took advantage of the options available to them.

"Would you like to wait by the fire while I check us in?" Steven asked.

Genevieve nodded and headed for the inviting fireplace on the right side of the lobby. She settled into a brown leather chair beside the warm fire and put up her feet on the raised hearth.

The motif of the New Brighton was definitely Northwest lodge. However, it was "lodge" décor in its most elegant form. The furniture in the lobby was oversized with an emphasis on polished wood and thick brown leather. A canoe hung from the ceiling, and a real pine tree grew out of the entryway's center. Only on the wild coast of Oregon would such a lodge feel natural.

"You look like you found a good spot." Steven joined Genevieve by the fire. He stood in front of the hearth, examining the mantle as if trying to figure out how it was attached. "This looks like cherry wood. Is that what you would guess?"

Genevieve had no idea. About the only types of wood she recognized were maple and oak. The tables she had ordered for the café were maple. She had set aside Leah's idea of filling the café with random sizes, shapes, and colors of tables and had decided on sturdy, round, maple tables. Lauren at the antique store had loaned Genevieve a stack of furniture catalogs and helped her to place the order earlier that afternoon. The chairs concerned her a bit because they didn't look as sturdy as the ones that came with the oak tables. But the price was right.

"What do you think, Gena? Cherry wood?"

"I guess. I'm not sure." She realized she had already violated her decision to relax and not to worry about the café or anything else.

"I made dinner reservations for us at six-thirty. How does that sound?"

Genevieve checked her watch. It was already 6:20. "Is it a formal dining room?"

"I'm sure what you're wearing is fine. As a matter of fact, I like that outfit on you. I was going to say something earlier. That's a good color on you. Is it new?"

"No." Genevieve glanced at her sweater. It was a pale lavender shade and was at least two years old. Was it possible Steven had never seen it on her? Or had he just not noticed or said anything when she wore it in the past?

"It's fine with me if we go directly to dinner now." Genevieve rose from her chair.

"Actually, why don't you wait here?" Steven suggested. "I'll make sure our luggage made it to our room and come right back."

Genevieve settled into the chair once again and told herself to relax. She discretely slipped off her shoes and let the fire's warmth penetrate her cold feet. Wiggling her toes, she stared into the flames. Slender branches of golden fire stretched from the fat logs, swaying in an unseen draft.

I wonder why Steven wanted to come here this weekend. This isn't routine for him. Usually he only wants to go away for our anniversary weekend.

Genevieve remembered that the last time they had tried to get away was for their twenty-fifth wedding anniversary. Steven had made all the plans for them to go to Hawaii for a week. They got into a huge argument on the way to the airport and had a miserable flight to Oahu. A terrible storm was dumping buckets of rain on the Hawaiian Islands when they arrived, and they spent the first two days in their hotel room barely speaking to each other. They called a truce by the end of the second day, and the rest of their anniversary week was cordial and uneventful.

Genevieve didn't know what to expect this weekend. For a flitter of a moment, she wondered if Steven had some announcement to make to her and wanted to be away from home when he told her.

There I go, fretting again. Why can't I be at peace about any- thing? Where is all this anxiety coming from?

Steven appeared and offered her his hand. They walked quietly through the lobby to the dining room. Their table was next to the floor-to-ceiling windows that faced the ocean. The sun already had gone down, and the rain splat- tering against the windows smeared their limited view of the outside world. It was cold sitting near the glass. Genevieve studied the menu while wiggling her toes in an effort to pro- long the fire's warming effects.

Dining out was something Genevieve enjoyed. She liked

to evaluate the items listed on the menu and see how chefs used common ingredients with uncommon results.

The soup of the day caught her eye. It was lobster bisque. Both she and Steven started with a cup of soup, followed with a spinach salad garnished with pecans and mandarin orange slices. Their conversation was light, as it had been in the car on the forty-minute drive to the coast.

"I know you told me that Mallory is staying with the Johnsons," Steven said. "But did I ask you where Anna ended up this weekend?"

He had asked in the car, but Genevieve's answer must not have stuck with him. "Anna is at a sleepover with some girls from the church. They're at Brad and Alissa's house."

Steven knew Brad and Alissa well because they both had been renters at the duplex next to Steven and Genevieve's home in Pasadena.

"What is Anna doing tomorrow?" Steven asked.

"She's going to stay at Brad and Alissa's and help them get the room ready for the girls."

"That's right," Steven said. "The time is getting pretty close for them, isn't it? When do they go to Russia to pick up the girls?"

"It's Romania, actually." Genevieve pushed the rest of her soup aside. It wasn't very warm, and the flavors had been a disappointment. She preferred to save room for the salad and the main course of cedar-grilled salmon with a glaze of brown sugar and cilantro. "The adoption of the two sisters was final a few weeks ago, but they're waiting for all the paperwork from the government to come through."

"How old will the girls be when they arrive?"

"Two and almost three. There's only eleven months between them."

"Almost like having twins," Steven said. "Brad and Alissa are certainly going to see their lives change."

Genevieve nodded. "Children do have that effect on you."

Steven seemed thoughtful a moment. "I don't think our lives changed much after our girls were born, do you?"

Genevieve clenched her teeth. All her efforts to remain relaxed flew out the window, and before she could hold back her words, she stated, "You would have to have been around to notice."

Steven put down his fork. Genevieve knew the signal. From the look in his eye, she knew he was weary yet nonetheless willing to meet her on the other side of the line she had just drawn in the sand.

"You knew what my career entailed when you married me."

"I was nineteen, Steven. I didn't know anything."

"You knew plenty, Genevieve. Why is it that we can never resolve this issue? What is it you blame me for?"

"I don't blame you for anything. You've made a wonderful life for the girls and me."

"That's not true. You still blame me for losing all that money in the stock market, don't you?"

Both of them spoke in low, constrained voices. No one in the restaurant would have known they were fighting.

"That's all in the past, Steven. We can't keep looking

back." Genevieve smoothed the stiff linen of the cloth napkin in her lap. The bitterness she had harbored for so long
against Steven had become a tangled vine, winding through
her heart's garden. Many times she thought she had hacked
away at the source of the problem, only to find that what
had been removed was just a branch and not the root.

Without thinking about it, Genevieve let words slip
through her lips. "Besides, you had a choice. You could have
put all the money in the bank."

Steven leaned closer. "You *are* still holding it against me,
aren't you? You think I talked you into making the stock
market investment."

"You were the one who did all the research and had the
hot lead."

"You could have disagreed at any point, and I would
have dropped the whole idea."

"I know. It was a mutual decision. We did what we
thought was best. I don't hold the decision against you." Her
words were bloodless, robotic, and void of life.

"Yes, we did what we thought was best. For you. For us.
For your dad's money. Your father would have understood.
He would have, Gena. Do you still think he is somehow
angry with you?"

Genevieve didn't answer. She thought back to their wedding day and how her father barely spoke to her because he
was angry that she was marrying an American. He had performed his duty, walking her down the aisle the same way
he had performed his duty of walking her to school every
day. She desperately yearned for him to offer a warm

squeeze of her hand or a kiss on the cheek before he turned her over to Steven at the altar. Instead, her father had given her a stiff half-bow from the waist just as he had done for years at the school yard's gate.

In her mind that day had pounded his admonition, "Make something of your life that will shine brightly." By marrying an American and interrupting her university education, her father no longer believed she could make anything bright or promising of her life.

Then her father had turned, sat down beside her mother, and folded his arms. Genevieve stepped up to the altar, put her hand in Steven's, and somehow transferred all that pain and disappointment into their marriage.

Now Steven reached for Genevieve's hand across the table and said with steady, even words, "Gena, this needs to get settled. I'm not perfect. Nobody is. Your father wasn't perfect, either. He's gone now."

"And so is his money."

"Yes, and so is his money. We've been over this before. There's nothing we can do to change that loss, Gena. I'm trying my best here. When will you believe me when I tell you I love you? I'm here for you. I always have been."

Genevieve's eyes narrowed as she looked into Steven's sincere face. "When are you here for me? You're leaving again Monday. You're not here, Steven. You're never here."

Steven sighed and leaned back, as if her blow had hit its intended mark. "Yes, I am leaving Monday. That's my job. My job that I love and you hate. I've paid my dues for your resentment of my career. We moved to Glenbrooke, like you wanted. We took another risk with the rest of the inheritance money and bought the café, like you wanted. What more do you want, Genevieve? Tell me, because I really would like to know."

The waiter stepped up to the table at that moment, clearing their soup bowls and serving their salads. Genevieve had lost her appetite. She stared at one of the mandarin orange slices and tried to breathe slowly.

In a small voice she said, "I don't want anything from you."

"You know what?" Steven said. "There's something I want from you."

Genevieve looked up. She hadn't expected his statement.

"I know you didn't ask me what I wanted from you, but I'll tell you anyway. I want you to forgive me."

"Forgive you for what?"

Steven sat back. He pressed his thumb to his cheek and rested his fingers across his mouth as if deep in thought. "Only you can answer that, Genevieve. You say all these mistakes of mine are in the past, and yet I feel as if every single mistake I've ever made hangs around my neck like an invisible weight."

"I don't hold anything against you, Steven," she said quickly. "And I don't think it has anything to do with my father. Both he and Mom loved you like a son before they died. They knew you were a good husband and father. And you are. I don't hold anything against you. I'm sorry I brought up the money. It doesn't matter. It's in the past. I don't want to ever discuss it again."

"I wish I could believe that," Steven said.

They remained silent for a solid three minutes while they ate their salads. Genevieve hated the way she felt right now. Something needed to change. The darkness inside her spirit was smothering her. She had lost all sense of what was true and what was a deception.

Steven cleared his throat and held out a verbal olive branch before Genevieve's barricaded heart. "We have a whole weekend ahead of us. I don't want to argue with you. I want both of us to enjoy the time we have together."

Genevieve forced a weak smile, as she had so many other times when their battle reached this point. "I don't want to argue with you, either."

Steven reached across the table and squeezed her hand. Genevieve knew that she would now do what she had done often before. She would retreat deep inside herself and leave only a shadow of the true Genevieve holding Steven's hand and accompanying him through the rest of the weekend.

Little had changed inside Genevieve, despite their truce. The heaviness of her deepening sadness hung on her spirit like an overgrown vine blocking the light and air. There was no way on this green earth that she could get this darkness off her. She had tried before and nothing worked.

The only thing that helped was when she immersed herself so deeply in a project that no room was left for vine chopping. She survived by doing, not by brooding.

With renewed determination, Genevieve focused on all the good things she could find in Steven and in their marriage. This would be her project during the weekend. She would think about only positive aspects or their life together and do all she could to make her time with Steven wonderful. Brooding would not be allowed this weekend.

When the sun came out Saturday, the two of them took an afternoon drive down the coast. Genevieve tied a turquoise scarf around her neck and let the wind tie her hair in tangles. She drank in the fresh sea air as if it were an elixir. They drove for miles without speaking. The space and air and time gave Genevieve a chance to downshift.

After a decadently delicious crème brûlée at a French restaurant, Genevieve slipped her hand into her husband's as they walked out the door to the parking lot. Steven opened the car door for her. Before she got in, she kissed him generously. Her decision to focus on the positive was having a good effect on her.

On the way home Sunday afternoon, Genevieve felt refreshed. She told Steven they should do this more often, and she admitted she needed to get away more than she had realized.

"That's what the girls told me," Steven said.

Genevieve asked what he meant.

"Anna and Mallory told me you've been working too hard at the café. Anna said she thought the two of us needed to spend some time with each other away from all that."

"This weekend was Anna's idea?"

"No, it was my idea. But Anna's comments prompted me to put the plans all together. I guess I needed to hear from the girls how hard you've been working."

Immediately an old, familiar accusation flew to

Genevieve's mind. *You wouldn't need them to report to you about my life if you were actually around to live it with me.*

Genevieve determinedly pushed back the wave of anger that threatened to crash over her. She told herself not to think about the negative. Steven was here with her now. He had been with her all weekend. It had been a restful weekend in which the real Genevieve had almost begun to integrate with the shadow of Genevieve who had started out the weekend with Steven.

The struggle was more intense than she expected. By the time they arrived home, Genevieve had slipped back into the familiar place of darkness and discouragement deep inside her heart. She hid behind her well-rehearsed role of attentive mother and careful homemaker. The girls seemed happy that their mother had glowing reports about the great time she had enjoyed with their father. Anna and Mallory seemed to have no trouble believing all their mother's words were true.

But this time, Genevieve knew that Steven wasn't buying it.

Chapter Six

Genevieve arrived early for work Monday and noticed that Leah had installed the awning. It looked exactly as Genevieve had hoped it would. The outside appeal of the Wildflower Café was now as perfect as it could be.

Inside, the brighter lights helped a little. The café was about half full of customers. Leah, who had donned her baseball cap that morning, was making the rounds with a coffeepot.

"Hey," Leah greeted Genevieve, "how was the romantic weekend getaway?"

"Very nice." Genevieve was aware that everyone in the café could hear her answer. "After all that rain on Friday, Saturday was beautiful on the coast."

"We had a high of sixty-eight degrees here," one of the elderly gentlemen at table number three said.

"Time to get some corn in the ground, now that the rains have let up," another man said.

Leah began to discuss gardening techniques with the men while Genevieve slipped into the kitchen and pulled a clean apron from the drawer. It felt good to be back. This was her domain, and she was full of plans for improvement. With Steven gone for a week, she could concentrate on the girls and the Wildflower Café with renewed energy.

Her momentum, however, came to a dead stop two days later when Leah handed her the phone and said, "It's the delivery service for the new tables."

Genevieve listened while she stirred the day's soup in a large kettle. She couldn't believe what the man was telling her.

"No," Genevieve answered him, "it would not be okay for you to deliver the tables Friday. As I explained when I ordered them, I need them today because all of the old tables are being removed today."

"I wish I could help you," the man on the other end of the line said. "But like I said, we've had some delivery complications here at the warehouse, and the absolute soonest I can get the two tables to you is by Friday."

"It's not two tables; it's twelve tables."

The man paused before saying, "On the order form here, I don't see a one before the two. Are you sure you ordered twelve tables?"

"Yes, I ordered twelve tables and four chairs for each table."

"I'm sorry, ma'am, but according to the paperwork I

have, you only ordered two tables. I'll have to call you back after I've checked the original order form."

Genevieve let out an exasperated huff as she hung up the phone.

"Everything okay?" Leah slipped into the kitchen and scooped up two lunch plates.

"No. The order for the tables and chairs is a shambles!"

Leah paused. "Should I tell Seth not to come with the delivery truck this afternoon?"

"I don't know. I don't want to let Shelly down. She needs the tables for her May Day event Saturday."

"Which reminds me," Leah said. "I have to talk to you about that. Let me serve these lunches, and I'll be right back."

Genevieve prepared a tuna sandwich and a chicken salad sandwich while waiting for Leah to return. Leah served the prepared sandwiches and then bustled back through the swinging door. "About the May Day event. Would it help if I took some of the food over Friday evening and set up things in the camp kitchen? I told Shelly I'd help her with table decorations, and I thought I might as well take the food when I go."

"Yes, that would be very helpful. Thanks, Leah."

"No problem. And let me know as soon as you find out about the new tables so I can give Seth a call."

By that afternoon, Genevieve still didn't know what she was going to do about the tables. The furniture warehouse hadn't called back so she knew she would have to pursue them. Business had slowed down. Only four women sat in the dining room at the corner table. They were sipping tea and sharing desserts.

Genevieve decided to use the phone in the dining room so she could sit down as she spoke to the delivery service and have all the information in front of her. She also thought it might help her to control her temper and to be more polite since the young women sitting at the window table could overhear her if they wanted to.

One of the women at the table, Jessica Buchanan, looked up and greeted Genevieve from across the room with a smile and a wave. Jessica, a gentle-spirited mother of three, had initiated this meeting time at the Wildflower Café a few weeks ago so several women could participate, without their toddlers, in an informal Bible study. The group previously had met at Jessica's beautiful Victorian home. Genevieve had been invited numerous times to join them, but she had declined the invitations over the months, saying that her work schedule was too busy.

At least, that was the reason Genevieve gave. The real reason was that she was nervous about making a commitment to keep up with the study. Years ago, when she had jumped into Bible Study Fellowship with both feet, she had been searching for answers and direction in her life. Now she was hiding. Hiding from her husband, from herself, and although she hadn't admitted it yet, hiding from God beneath the tangled vines in her heart's garden. The last place she wanted to be was around women who were out in the open.

"Yes, this is Genevieve Ahrens calling back for…" She

checked the warehouse invoice in front of her. "Is it Jack?"

"One moment please." A click was followed by music while Genevieve was put on hold. Of all things, the music was Christmas carols!

She held the phone far enough away from her ear not to be bowled over by the sound of sweet silver bells. Without intending to, Genevieve heard every word the women in the Bible study group were saying.

"My favorite verse in this chapter is definitely verse 6," one of the women said. She had warm, brown skin and thick, curly, brown hair that fell over her shoulders. Genevieve had seen her in the café before, and she knew it was possible she had met her, but Genevieve couldn't remember her name.

"It seems so crazy," the woman said, "that Jesus would walk up to this man, who is lying there, paralyzed, and ask him, 'Do you want to be made well?' I mean, what paralyzed person wouldn't want to be healed?"

Genevieve heard the music stop and held the phone up to her ear. "Hello?" It was only a pause on the music track. Strains of "Feliz Navidad" came pounding through the receiver louder than the silver bells had been. She turned the phone away and listened to the women with her back to them.

"I wrote down verse 6 as my key verse, too," another woman said. "Why do you think Jesus asked the paralyzed man if he wanted to be healed?"

"I thought about it a lot, and I asked Gordon—"

One of the women cut in. "No fair getting input from

husbands when they're pastors!"

The other women laughed.

Genevieve remembered the identity of the woman with the warm brown skin. Her name was Teri, and her husband was the new pastor at Glenbrooke Community Church. Leah had been talking about Teri and Gordon ever since they had arrived from Hawaii. Genevieve knew all about how Teri had taught at the high school with Jessica years ago and how Teri and her Australian husband had twin boys in kindergarten and a baby girl. They were living temporarily with Jessica and her husband, Kyle, since the Buchanan mansion on Madison Hill was large enough to be a hotel.

Genevieve wondered what a pastor's wife would say about wanting to be made well. After all, Genevieve knew what it was like to be stuck in a paralyzed state emotionally. She had been that way a long time. No one had ever asked her if she wanted to be well.

"Gordo and I got into a big discussion about how sometimes we get stuck in our lives and in our routines." Teri's voice carried across the room as clearly as if she were speaking directly to Genevieve. "The paralyzed man in John 5 certainly had the routine down pat. He spent every day at the same place, doing the same thing, with the same blind and lame people."

"You know what?" Jessica said. "Excuse me for interrupting, but it doesn't specifically say that this man was paralyzed. It just says that he had an infirmity for thirty-eight years."

"You're right," Teri said. "I hadn't noticed that. It doesn't specify his particular problem, which makes this verse even more applicable to my life and what I was going to say. This man had been in this same routine with his problem, whatever it was, for thirty-eight years. Jesus comes to him, asks if he wants to be made well, and instead of simply saying yes, the guy gives the excuse that no one will help him."

Another woman spoke up. "And then Jesus heals him anyhow, right there, regardless of his excuse."

"Yes, exactly," Teri said. "That's why I marked this verse. I think it's possible to have an infirmity of some sort and live with it as a routine for decades. It's possible to forget that Jesus Christ has the power and the desire to heal us. We just find excuses and keep living with things as they've always been. But He is such an incredible, loving Father that He overlooks our weakness, even our inability to respond to Him correctly. He looks right at the heart, and He…"

"Y-ello. This is Jack." The voice on the other end of the phone jolted Genevieve back to the task before her. She felt her neck turning red and her cheeks burning.

"Yes, um." Genevieve cleared her throat and tried to collect her thoughts. "I, um, this is…I spoke with you earlier. This is Genevieve Ahrens. I'm calling back about the order for the maple tables and chairs."

"Right," Jack said.

"Were you able to find the correct order for twelve and not two tables?"

"I checked with several people on that order, and it looks as if the salesman made the mistake when he checked the inventory. We don't have twelve tables in that style anywhere on the West Coast. The only other distribution center that carries that set is located in South Carolina, but it only has one set left. It's a discontinued model. I don't know if the sales rep told you that."

"No, he didn't."

"What would you like me to do about your order? We can ship two tables out to you by Friday, but it would take at least ten days to get the other table from the East Coast."

"That's still only three tables."

"That's right."

"Then I'd like to cancel my order," Genevieve said as calmly as she could. "I'll call the salesman who placed the order and tell him I've authorized you not to deliver the tables to me Friday."

"I sure am sorry about the mix-up."

"I am, too." Genevieve hung up the phone with a sickening feeling in her stomach. Dialing the number for the salesman, she tried to center all her attention on the problem at hand, even though part of her wanted to fly over to the table where the women were discussing the Bible. Her thirst for truth and encouragement was overpowering.

Focus on this project.

She knew the aching in her spirit would subside if she could divert her attention and dive into a huge project. It always worked in the past. Today, it was difficult.

She made the call, left a brief phone message for the salesman explaining the problem, and asked him to call her back. Then she bent her head over the file folder, as if studying the order form. She really was listening to the women, half afraid to hear any more yet not able to turn away. To her disappointment, they had concluded their discussion.

"Before we close," Jessica said, "I was wondering what the rest of you thought about adding half an hour to our meeting time. This hour went too fast."

The others agreed, and the time was set for two-thirty next Wednesday at the Wildflower Café. Then Jessica prayed. Genevieve kept her head bowed over her order form with her pen in her hand and her eyes opened slightly. She loved listening to Jessica pray.

With earnest words she asked for God's blessing on the women gathered at the table. She prayed for their husbands and their children, and then she added words that seemed to sweep across the room and wrap their arms around Genevieve.

"Thank You for bringing Genevieve and her family to Glenbrooke. Father, bless her for all she has done in providing this wonderful place for us to meet. I thank You for the way You have used her to renew the hope of so many by bringing beauty into our little downtown area. Please give her Your peace and Your joy. I pray this in the name of Your Son, Jesus Christ, who is the great healer of our lives. Amen."

With her heart pounding wildly, Genevieve rose from her table and slipped into the kitchen. The light from these women was too bright. All she wanted to do was go back into hiding.

Genevieve wasn't alone when she entered the kitchen. Leah was talking to Brad, who had come over from his computer store next door.

"Hey, Gena," Brad greeted her. "How's it going?"

"Hi, Brad. I'm okay. How about you?"

Brad Phillips had recently gotten his hair cut shorter than Genevieve had ever seen it in the six years she had known him. She guessed he was trying to get used to the role of respectable father of two toddlers that he would soon be experiencing.

"We just had a power failure next door," Brad said. "I'm surprised your electricity didn't go off as well. I reset all the circuit breakers, but that didn't do any good. I think I overloaded all the old wiring once and for all. I made a couple of calls on your phone. My lines are all goofed up."

Leah held out the last crumbled slice of chocolate cake on a plate to Brad with a fork. "What are you going to do?"

"Pray," Brad said before shoveling the first bite of cake into his mouth.

Genevieve knew his answer was serious. Brad and Alissa had become very serious about praying ever since they decided to adopt the two girls from Romania. The process had taken more than ten months so far, and they made it known that they were praying their way through every day of it.

When the couple had arrived in Glenbrooke several years ago, Alissa had opened a travel agency next to the café called A Wing and a Prayer. Her logo was a globe with two angel-like wings. Brad expanded the idea when Alissa and Brad switched offices, and he opened up his computer shop while she moved her office home. Brad's business logo was a computer sporting little wings and tilted upward, as if flying off to heaven. He welcomed defunct computers that were ready to "wing their way to oblivion." He had customers sign a document that said they were willing for their ailing units to be "organ donors." Brad offered the customers credit for software and then he cannibalized the old computers. The old parts fed his on-line business of providing and shipping spare parts of outdated computers all over the world. That was how he and Alissa first connected with the orphanage in Romania.

"This is delicious." Brad took another bite of cake.

"We call it Meri's Midnight Madness," Leah said. "The recipe came from Shelly's sister, Meredith. It's made with dark chocolate and mayonnaise. Isn't it good?"

"There's mayonnaise in this?" Brad said. "You're kidding!"

Genevieve reminded herself never to tell the men what went into the desserts.

"What happened with the order for the tables, Gena?" Leah asked.

Genevieve explained the situation, and Brad said, "Why didn't you tell me? I can order you tables. I can get you anything you need. Or at least once I have power back so I can go on-line. How many tables do you want?"

Genevieve showed Brad her order form with the style of maple tables she originally had ordered. "At this point, I think I'd rather spend more to buy the oak tables, but I don't want to have to deal with the same company anymore."

"Got it." Brad put his empty plate down on the counter. He pulled out a pen and made a few notes in the margins of

Genevieve's order form. "Mind if I take this with me?"

"Sure, that's fine."

"When do you want the tables delivered?"

"Tomorrow?" Genevieve's expression echoed the question in her voice.

Leah explained about how the old tables were needed by Shelly for the May Day weekend.

"How about this," Brad suggested. "Why don't you tell Shelly the tables are on loan until your new ones arrive? I'll help Seth take them over to the camp for May Day, but we can do that Friday, can't we?"

"What will we use for tables at the café Saturday?" Leah asked.

"You could close for the day," Brad suggested. "Half the women in Glenbrooke will be at Camp Heather Brook anyway. Or set up folding tables. It's not Pasadena, Gena. People around here will understand if you have to wing it for a few days. We have a card table you can use."

"I have two," Leah said. "That's a good idea, Brad. We'll get creative with some tablecloths, and I would guess most customers will barely notice."

Brad's idea worked out better than Genevieve thought it would. By the time she and the girls headed home late Friday night, all the catered food had been prepared for Saturday's event at Camp Heather Brook, and the dining room was a colorful hodgepodge of card tables covered with a variety of cloths. Some of the tablecloths came from Genevieve's stash at home, and a few came from the salvaged stack of linens they had pulled from the storage shed weeks earlier.

"Do we have to go out to the camp now?" Mallory asked once they were in the car.

"No, Leah took all the food over there an hour ago. She's going early tomorrow morning to prepare the food in the camp kitchen. That's why I need the two of you to help me serve breakfast here tomorrow morning. We're closing at ten-thirty, and that's when the three of us will go to Camp Heather Brook."

"We're going to miss the brunch part," Mallory said.

"Yes, but we'll be there for the rest of the fun. Last year the May Day event went until after two o'clock."

"I hope they have a craft again this year," Mallory said. "That was my favorite part last year."

"Mom, can we stop at Dairy Queen on the way home?" Anna asked from the passenger's seat. "I'm starving."

Genevieve glanced over at her fourteen-year-old. "How can you be starving? Plenty of food was available to you at the Wildflower for the past five hours!"

"I know, but I didn't want any of that food. Do you mind? I'm really hungry for French fries, and you don't serve French fries at the café."

"Me, too," Mallory piped up from the backseat. "I haven't had French fries in forever. Could we please stop, Mom?"

Genevieve gave in. Anna and Mallory had been real troopers, setting up tables, sweeping the floor, and even cleaning the restroom. She drove several miles out of her way to Dairy Queen and restrained from giving any lectures on nutrition.

The hamburgers, shakes, and fries her daughters soon held in their laps made them giddy with appreciation.

"I don't think you've ever taken us to Dairy Queen." Mallory slurped her strawberry shake.

"Of course I have."

"I don't remember when you ever did," Mallory said. "Dad always takes us there. He orders a peanut butter blizzard."

Genevieve didn't know that. Steven liked ice cream, but she never would have guessed he had a favorite blizzard flavor, especially not peanut butter.

"When does Dad get home?" Anna asked.

"Sunday," Genevieve said. The proclamation didn't bring joy to her the way it did to the girls. She felt as if this time when Steven left she had gone into a deeper place of suspended emotions. She barely had thought of Steven or wondered about him during the five days he had been gone. It was as if he were so separated from her everyday life that he existed as only a memory. She assumed that she and the girls were also a suspended memory for him while he was gone.

Genevieve found three messages waiting for her on voice mail when she got home. One was from Leah reminding her that if Mr. Olestrum came in for breakfast, like he usually did on Saturday mornings, Genevieve was supposed to use the egg substitute instead of real eggs because his wife was watching his cholesterol, but he wasn't supposed to know he was being served egg substitute.

With a grin, Genevieve erased the message. The next one was from her eldest daughter, Josephina. Fina's voice bubbled over with excitement. She had gotten the job she wanted with a sports club a mile from her apartment in Arizona. As soon as her classes ended in three weeks, she would begin to teach summer volleyball clinics.

Genevieve leaned against the kitchen counter and listened to Fina's message again. She sounded so happy.

The realization that Genevieve wouldn't see her twenty-one-year-old daughter for several more months entered her heart like a previously unknown variety of pain. She was delighted, of course, that Fina got the job and that she could spend the summer in Arizona the way she wanted. But Genevieve was now separated even further from a part of herself; her firstborn was truly on her own.

Genevieve saved the message. She had a feeling she would need to hear her daughter's voice again later and be reminded of how excited Fina was about the job. This strain of reality would take a while to soak in.

The third message on her voice mail was from Steven. "Good news," he said. "My schedule was changed. I'm in San Francisco now. I'm on standby to catch the next flight home. It might be as late as three o'clock tomorrow afternoon before I can get there. Maybe sooner. Oh, and Gena, I have twenty-three days off. We should be able to get to some of that yard work you've been wanting to do once the weather cooperated. I love you, Gena. Give my love to the girls. See you soon."

Steven sounded happy to be coming home. He sounded just as happy about coming home as Fina was about not coming home.

Genevieve didn't know how she felt about anything or anyone anymore. All she knew was that the day had been full, and she was tired.

"Girls," Genevieve called down the hallway as she headed for her bedroom, "I'm taking a bath and going to bed. You both need to be in bed by ten o'clock at the very latest. Understand?"

"Yes, Mom."

"Good answer." Genevieve turned on the bath water. "I love it when they just say yes instead of coming up with a bunch of excuses."

She stopped and stared at her reflection in the bathroom mirror. *Yes. They said yes without any excuses. Where did I just hear someone talking about that?*

She took off her shoes, and then it came to her. *The Bible study at the Wildflower. That was Teri's observation about the man who was healed. He made excuses when Jesus asked if he wanted to be made well.*

All Genevieve's thoughts and feelings did something they rarely did. They mingled. It was as if all her feelings lined up on one side of the dance floor while all her thoughts stood stoically on the other. In her imagination she couldn't tell which one made the first move—whether it was a thought or a feeling—but suddenly they were mixing and mingling. Thoughts and feelings together on the same dance floor of her mind for the first time in ages. They seemed to all be in position, waiting for the music to begin.

Genevieve stared into the mirror, studying the dark flecks in the orbits of her gray irises. The whites of her eyes carried faint bloodshot streaks. The shadows under her eyes darkened as the steam rose from the tub and fogged the mirror. She was lost. Lost in herself. Hidden away.

She turned off the water, and in the split second of silence that followed, a distinct thought flashed through her mind. *Do you want to be made well, Genevieve?*

For a moment she stopped breathing. It was as if all the imaginary eyes on the dance floor in her mind were fixed on her, waiting for her answer. All her routine excuses hovered overhead, like balloons ready to drop at a New Year's party.

"Do I want to be made well?" Genevieve repeated aloud. She realized that she hadn't asked herself if she *needed* to be made well. That was a conclusion she had come to some time ago. Something was definitely wrong in her life and needed to be repaired.

But she had fought hard to ignore that conclusion.

Before a single excuse "balloon" could drop, Genevieve looked into the still water that now filled her bathtub. "Yes." She heard herself whisper without hesitation. "Yes, I want to be made well."

Chapter Seven

An orchestra didn't suddenly come alive in Genevieve's mind when she stated that she wanted to be made well. Her feelings and thoughts didn't let out a cheer and begin to dance together in a gleeful frenzy, as she half-expected. Instead, everything went quiet. All the images evaporated, and in their place a strange, settling peace came over her.

Her request to be made well was the first bit of a prayer that she had uttered in a long time. More than a prayer, it was a response. The unusual peace that came with her response was profound.

She lowered herself into the tub and drew in a deep breath, then another. Her lungs filled with the warm, moist air as she tried to make sense of what had just happened.

Was that God's voice or my splintered psyche?

He called me by my name.

Or did He?

Did God just heal me?

Just like that?

What exactly did He heal me from?

I know something has been wrong for a long time, but I don't know exactly what it is.

How can God heal me when I don't even know what my "infirmity" is?

Genevieve had difficulty identifying what she felt. She still didn't feel excited about seeing Steven tomorrow. The long list of past hurts didn't seem to have been lifted from her heart.

The settling peace that had come to her presided over her thoughts, not her feelings. Her mind was able to rest. Her heart, however, was still a locked fortress.

After her soothing bath, Genevieve went to bed and slept deeply. In the middle of the night, the phone rang. She stumbled out of bed and reached for the phone.

"Is this Genevieve Ahrens?" the woman's voice on the other end asked.

"Yes." She squinted at the display on the alarm clock. It was 4:37.

"I'm calling from the Glenbrooke Emergency Dispatch. We sent out a fire unit to Main Street approximately one hour ago. One of our volunteers, Kyle Buchanan, asked that I call you."

"A fire?" Genevieve was jolted wide awake.

"I don't have any details yet. Kyle wanted you to go down right away."

"Yes. Okay. Thank you." Hanging up and flipping on the

light switch, Gena fumbled with a pair of jeans and pulled a fleece sweatshirt on over her pajama top. She woke the girls and hustled them into the car with her. They peppered her with questions all the way, but Genevieve had no answers for them until she turned down Main Street and saw the fire engine pulling away from the front of the café.

"I can smell the smoke, Mom," Anna said as Genevieve parked the car. "Should we get out?"

"No, let's wait a minute." Genevieve anxiously peered into the darkness. The front of the café seemed unaffected. The awning, bicycle, and flowerboxes all looked fine in the streetlight's dim glow. "It might be all right," she said. "A false alarm, maybe."

"Can't we get out, Mom?" Mallory asked. "We won't go in or anything."

"No, honey." Genevieve rolled down her window. The smell of smoke became overpowering. "Let's wait a minute."

She recognized Kyle's truck parked at the end of Main Street. He appeared around the corner of the building wearing full firefighting gear.

"He's waving for us to come over there." Anna opened her door.

"Okay, stay with me, girls."

"We will, Mom. Don't worry," Anna said.

As soon as they neared the café, they noticed the shattered glass on the sidewalk. The heat from the fire apparently had blown out the windows. The glass shards looked like frozen, sharp-sided snowflakes resting on the flowers and the sidewalk.

"Oh, Mom." Anna pointed to the black soot smears that shot up the front of the building. "Look."

In her shock at the sight, Genevieve thought for a moment that if the windows were the eyes of the café, then the smoke was like great smudges of mascara. Her Wildflower Café had been crying. And she hadn't been there.

Kyle met them and reached for Genevieve's hand, giving it a squeeze. "I'm so sorry to be the one to break this to you, Gena. I thought it might help if you got here now rather than later this morning."

"How bad is it?"

"The kitchen is gone," Kyle said.

Genevieve held her breath.

"And the dining room sustained enough smoke and water damage that I have a feeling the insurance will consider it a complete loss."

Genevieve felt as if the whole world suddenly tilted to the left.

"The bicycle is fine." Anna examined her contribution to the café with care.

"Can we see inside?" Mallory slipped her hand into her mom's.

"Yes, I'll take you around to the back." Kyle turned on a large flashlight.

"Any idea what started it?" Genevieve asked. "I'm sure I turned off the oven and stove."

"It was the wiring," Kyle said. "This is an old building, as you know. It appears some smoldering was going on for a while with the wires inside the wall."

Genevieve remembered Brad's experiencing a power failure the day before. "Was Brad's shop affected?"

"Somewhat, but not nearly as bad as the café. The initial problem might have been on Brad's side of the common wall, but the fire broke through on your side, in the kitchen. We probably won't be able to evaluate the extent of Brad's loss until he has a chance to look at everything. He should be here pretty soon."

From the view afforded them by the light of Kyle's flashlight, the kitchen looked like a ghastly black-and-white negative of what had only hours ago been Genevieve's sparkling clean workspace. A gaping hole was in the backdoor where the firefighters hacked through with an ax, leaving jagged, splintered boards in their wake. All the hanging pots and pans above the stove were charred and distorted. Part of the counter was completely gone, melted into great stalagmites of foul-smelling plastics. The wall to the right was burned down, exposing the tiny bathroom where the metal paper towel dispenser stuck out like a blackened wart on the disfigured face of the only wall still standing. Chunks of the roof opened to the celestial darkness overhead.

"This is awful," Anna said solemnly. "How can it look so perfect out front and be this demolished inside?"

"I suggest you get your insurance adjuster here first thing in the morning," Kyle said. "When you come back in the daylight, be sure to bring a camera to record the damage as it is right now."

"Okay," Genevieve answered numbly. "Is there anything else I should do?"

"I know it's hard, but try to keep your eyes on God and not on this situation." The gentleness in Kyle's tone washed over Genevieve, giving her a faint sense of comfort. Mostly she felt numb.

"God is still in control," Kyle said. "He gives us beauty for our ashes, you know. I see it happen all the time."

Genevieve nodded, but her insides had gone cold. She tried to think of her insurance agent's name, but it escaped her. She tried to recall what kind of policy she had finally settled on, but she couldn't remember. Her frantic thoughts jumped to the kitchen utensils that Leah had donated to the Wildflower. They were destroyed. How could she possibly replace all those gifts?

"Are you all right?" Kyle asked.

"Not really." She felt too overwhelmed to cry.

"If Jess and I can do anything, you call us, okay?"

Genevieve nodded. "I guess all I can do now is go home and start to make calls in a few hours."

"Mom," Mallory said, "you need to put a sign on the front door that says you're closed."

"I think people will figure that out," Anna said.

"We'll take care of all that," Kyle said. "You can go on home, if you want. It looks like Brad's car is pulling into the parking lot. I'll check on you later today."

"Thanks, Kyle."

"Sure. You remember to call if you need anything."

Genevieve was about to go when Brad and Alissa dashed

out of their car and joined Genevieve and Kyle. They all ended up spending the next half hour examining the damage by the light of Kyle's flashlight and discussing what caused the problem.

"I should have had the wires in the wall checked," Brad said for the seventh time. "I knew it was shorting out with all my additional equipment running off the power. I made far too many assumptions about the old wiring's capabilities."

"The café was pulling just as much power with the new appliances," Kyle said. "My guess is that the stress was equal from both sides."

"I find it astounding that the café sustained so much damage while our side was barely affected," Alissa said. Her shoulder-length, blond hair was pulled back in a clip so that it fanned out over the crown of her head like an ivory peacock tail. However, there was nothing proud or peacocklike about Alissa. She had a beautiful face. Even in the dim light, roused from bed, wearing no makeup, and full of concerned expressions, Alissa's looks would compel others to let their gazes linger.

"Mom, I'm getting cold." Mallory snuggled up next to Genevieve.

"We can go, honey," Genevieve said.

"I'll come by your house later this morning," Alissa said.

"Okay, thanks. And thank you, Kyle."

"Sure, don't mention it. I'm really sorry this happened to you."

"Yes, me, too." Genevieve walked to the car with one

arm around each of her daughters.

"At least the tables were at the camp," Anna said. "It will be easier to replace the card tables. Or at least it won't cost so much."

"Mmm-hmm."

"And like you told Alissa," Mallory added, "all the food for tomorrow was already at Camp Heather Brook. It would have been worse if the food had gotten burned up."

"Mmm-hmm."

"Remember last year, when you catered the May Day event, our oven didn't work?" Anna said. "That was a disaster."

"This was a worse disaster," Mallory said as they got into the car.

"Mmm-hmm."

The girls continued to express their opinions as Genevieve started the car and drove down silent Main Street. At the corner she turned left and noticed that the sun was beginning to illuminate the morning. Low, thin clouds padded the sky like strips of cotton gauze covering a wound.

Genevieve felt the throbbing of the wound in her heart at the loss of the café. Brad and the others had given lots of suggestions on how she could rebuild and how the café would be even better. None of them had paused long enough for Genevieve to mourn. Not that she blamed them. None of them had suffered the same degree of loss she had.

Why is it that I had such a definite spiritual moment last night by the tub, and then a few hours later my business is ruined? Did this happen because I told God I want to be made well? Why would He allow the only source of happiness in my life to be destroyed? He could have stopped this from happening. If God loves me, then—

"Mom, you missed the street to our house," Mallory chirped from the backseat.

Genevieve turned the car around and felt shivers of shock racing up her spine. The whole world seemed to be spinning out of control.

Why would God ask me if I want to be made well and then push me to the edge of a mental breakdown? Am I about to lose my mind?

Adjusting the rearview mirror, she examined her expression in the pale morning light. Her face looked normal. Distraught, yes. But not destroyed, like she felt inside. She looked fine. Except for her eyes. They stared back at a jagged angle and looked as if they were rimmed with dark soot smudges.

A frightening comparison flooded Genevieve's raw mind. The café is like my life. On the outside, from a distance, no one would know my marriage has any problems. But inside I've been smoldering for a painfully long time. Is that what God is trying to show me? Is my life about to fall into ruin?

She pulled into the driveway and pushed the button for the automatic garage door. The girls let out a cheer. Steven's sports car was parked inside the garage. He was home early.

Genevieve pulled into the garage and turned off the engine. Steven apparently heard them pulling in because he opened the backdoor. Still in uniform, he had a concerned expression on his face.

Genevieve could imagine how disturbed Steven must have felt when he came home to find the house empty.

For the first time in years, Genevieve ran to her husband, fell into his arms and wept.

For the next hour, Steven became the strongest rock Genevieve had ever leaned on. He comforted her and the girls and fixed them hot tea and toast while Genevieve talked on the phone to Leah and gave her all the details. Mallory and Anna went back to bed while Genevieve sat shivering on the living room couch.

Steven brought her a blanket and started a fire in the fireplace. He listened as she went over all the details for the third time. At last she stopped shivering.

"Can I bring you some more tea?" Steven asked.

"No, my stomach is too upset."

"Do you want to take a nap, or would it help if I tried to call the insurance company?"

"I don't think they'll be in the office before nine."

"Why don't you try to sleep for the next half hour or so? I'll wake you up at nine."

"Steven, I think I should tell you something."

He sat at the end of the couch, and she put her blanket-wrapped feet on his lap. Steven began to rub her feet.

"Something happened to me last night." Genevieve could feel her heart pounding. She rarely had talked to Steven about any of the events in her spiritual journey. In the past she assumed he wouldn't understand. Today she felt compelled to tell him what she had overheard Teri talking about at the café and how she turned off the bath water last night and sensed that the Lord was asking her if she wanted to be made well.

"I said yes," Genevieve said in a timid voice. "I don't know what it means. I don't even know why I'm telling you, but I thought something good was going to happen. I thought I'd feel better about myself and about our marriage. But the next thing I knew, the café was destroyed."

A fresh batch of tears welled up inside Genevieve. Her shoulders began to shake. "I don't feel better," she said before the first sob came over her. "I feel like everything is falling apart."

Steven's expression remained steady. He didn't tell her everything was going to be all right. He didn't say, "See? That's why I never put my trust in God." All he did was listen.

Genevieve tried hard to stop crying. "I don't understand what went wrong."

"I don't either," Steven said solemnly.

"I don't understand God."

"Neither do I."

They sat together in silence. Genevieve realized that was something her husband always had done well. He was good at being with her, listening to her, and supporting her through difficult situations. When he was home, he was 1000 percent home and 1000 percent with her.

What am I thinking? Steven is not *here for me. Isn't that what I've been saying all this time? How can I be sitting here thinking about how great it is that he's with me?*

"I'm going upstairs to bed," Genevieve said in a small

voice. "I think I need to get some sleep."

"Good idea," Steven said. "Would you like me to wake you at a certain time?"

"Wake me at ten o'clock, if I'm not up already."

Genevieve fell into her unmade bed and pulled the covers up to her chin. She closed her eyes and saw the ghastly, black charred remains of the Wildflower kitchen etched on the inside of her eyelids.

"My café," she whimpered in a low moan. "My dream café." Mercifully, exhaustion overtook her and silenced her with dreamless sleep.

Chapter Eight

*I*t took more than a month for all the paperwork to clear with the insurance company and for Genevieve to receive payment on the settlement for the café. The amount was almost double what she had expected thanks to Collin Radcliffe, a Glenbrooke lawyer who volunteered to assist her even after she insisted she didn't need help. Collin helped her to think of items she had forgotten to list on the original forms as well as what it would take to replace some of the built-in equipment at the current market price.

The stroke of brilliance that put Collin at the top of the list of local heroes was that he researched the history of the café's site. He discovered that section of Main Street originally had been the site of a library. In fact, it was the first library west of the Rockies that had been established in any logging town.

Genevieve failed to see why Collin grinned so broadly

when he delivered all the documents to her a week and a half after the fire. Then he opened a file, and it all became clear. Since the site was a historical landmark, they could apply for funds from not only the Oregon state government but also the federal government. Certain criteria had to be followed, such as the placement of a historical marker in front of the café.

The promise of additional funds for rebuilding the café launched Genevieve into a planning frenzy, and for almost a month she had dreamed bigger dreams than ever for the café. Having such a consuming project had a wonderful effect on her energy and contentment level. Steven was home and that made it easy for her to ignore her harbored anger toward him. They worked together with polite consideration.

The only time during the month after the fire that Genevieve felt a sense of panic was on the Wednesday right after the fire. She remembered that Jessica and her small circle of friends were to hold their Bible study that afternoon at two-thirty. All that morning Genevieve thought about Jessica and her group. It certainly wouldn't be a problem for them to meet at Jessica's large home, as they had done in the past.

But Genevieve struggled with the realization she wanted to be there with them. She wanted to hear what they had to say and inch her way back into a closer connection with God. She wanted to tell someone about her mysterious moment before her bath when she thought God was asking her if she wanted to be made well. She felt drawn to the light.

However, Genevieve's pride wouldn't allow her to call Jessica and say this was finally the day she could and would come.

The others will think I'm only turning back to God because the café was demolished.

I don't know what chapter they were studying during the week, so I won't have notes or thoughts to contribute to the discussion.

When the café is back up and running, I probably won't be able to continue with the group, so it's pointless to start something I can't finish.

Two-thirty came and went on that Wednesday, and Genevieve closed the door in her mind labeled "Jessica and the Bible study group." She pressed on with her plans to remodel the café more intensely than ever.

As the weeks went on, good-hearted, steady Steven stood with Genevieve, making few demands and even fewer complaints. He took extra time off so he could be available to her and the girls. He did extensive yard work and built shelves in the garage. He accompanied Mallory on her class field trip to the planetarium and drove Anna and two of her friends to the mall in Eugene. Steven and Genevieve spent most of their conversations discussing the girls and the café.

Five weeks after the fire an invitation came for their family to attend a special celebration for the arrival of Brad and Alissa's adopted daughters from Romania. The ceremony was to be held the second Sunday in June as part of the morning service. Out of the blue, Steven announced he wanted them to go, as a family, to show Brad and Alissa their support.

Genevieve was sitting at the kitchen table with a stack of papers when Steven walked in and stood beside her with a glass of iced tea in his hand.

"Did you see this in the mail?" Steven asked.

"No. Anna brought in the mail, but I haven't looked at any of it. My bookkeeping system has gotten a little behind." That morning the builder had asked Genevieve for a significant-sized check. She didn't have her accounts balanced yet and wasn't sure she could write the check.

That's when Steven showed her the invitation and made his announcement about the four of them attending church Sunday.

Genevieve put down her pen. "The event for the girls is being held at the church."

"I know."

"You've never gone to church before. For any reason."

"I know."

Genevieve examined her husband's calm face. "I'm sure Brad and Alissa will know that we support them even if we can't make it to the service."

"Why wouldn't we be able to go? I don't fly out until Tuesday. You don't have any scheduling conflicts, do you? The builders have Sunday off."

"It's just that…"

"What?"

Genevieve watched her husband's unchanging expression. It crossed her mind that he certainly was a good-looking man. Aside from his receding hairline and his fair skin, Steven's clear eyes and his distinctive, straight nose had changed little since the day she had met him. He had an aura of confidence that made her let out a deep breath and tell him honestly, "I feel funny going to church."

Steven waited for her to elaborate.

"I haven't been in months. I don't belong there. They have a new pastor. I don't even know him. It will be awkward."

Steven slowly sipped his tea and studied his wife. "You don't have to go. I'll take the girls. Anyone who asks about you will understand when I tell them you're buried under with details on the café."

Genevieve thought that statement certainly would be true, yet she felt unsettled down in her gut.

"Don't worry about it." Steven gently ran his thumb along her jaw. "You don't have to go to church if you're uncomfortable. I'll go with the girls."

Genevieve pressed her lips back in a smile. Steven bent over and gave her a soft kiss.

"I told Anna I'd pick her up from school and take her to Dairy Queen with a couple of her friends," he said. "I better get going. Mallory should be home pretty soon."

Genevieve nodded. Of course Mallory would be home soon. She knew the girls' schedules; he didn't need to tell her when her daughters got out of school.

Steven left with a wave over his shoulder. Genevieve turned and stared out the window at the improved landscape in the backyard. She knew she was looking at a labor of love that Steven had performed for her. He didn't care for yard work. That's why she had plunged in and done all the gardening in Pasadena. He also didn't need to pick up Anna or drive her around with her friends. But he was.

What was it that Leah said several months ago at the café? Something about how I'm always looking for the negative, and that's why I always find it.

She glanced down at the stack of invoices.

I'm never happy, am I? I have a faithful husband who could have left me at any time, but he hasn't. He cares deeply for the girls and me; we have three, healthy, beautiful daughters, a wonderful home. I have a chance to rebuild my dream café and enough money to make it what I want it to be, and I'm still miserable. What's wrong with me?

Genevieve didn't linger in her thoughts long enough to allow an answer to seep into her spirit. She had work to do. Books to balance. Checks to write. She picked up her reading glasses and tried to make out the faded print on one of the invoice copies. In the back of her mind, she heard Steven's voice. "You don't have to go to church if you're uncomfortable. I'll go with the girls."

Genevieve thought of all the years she had tried to get Steven to go to church with her in Pasadena. Never once did she say to him that he didn't have to go with her if he felt uncomfortable. Instead, she had needled him, begged him, shamed him, and finally had given up. Now he was the one who wanted to go to church, and she was the resistant one.

Genevieve yanked off her glasses. She leaned back in her chair, folded her arms, and said aloud, "Okay, what's going on here? My husband wants to go to church."

By Sunday morning, Genevieve had talked herself into going with Steven and the girls. She told herself it didn't matter what other people thought or how long it had been since she had gone. This was important to Brad, Alissa, and their new daughters.

As the four of them climbed into the car, the biggest knot Genevieve had ever experienced squeezed her left shoulder, giving her a painfully stiff neck. She pulled on her seatbelt and found she couldn't turn her head to check on the girls in the backseat.

"Wait," she said, as Steven was about to back out onto the driveway. "I need to run inside for one more thing."

"I got the card and the presents for the girls," Anna said.

"I know. I just need something." Genevieve hurried into the kitchen and opened the cupboard, searching for the strongest pain reliever they had. She swallowed two tablets with a quick glass of water and took the bottle with her.

"All set?" Steven didn't question what she had dropped from her clenched hand into her purse.

"Yes. Thanks for waiting."

They drove to Glenbrooke Community Church with Mallory chattering about how cute the youngest of the two Romanian sisters was. Genevieve hadn't seen the sisters during the five days they had been with Brad and Alissa, but she had heard from several people around town that they were pretty little girls.

"Beth has the biggest eyes," Mallory said. "You've never seen eyelashes this long on anybody. Beth is the little one.

Her sister is Ami. They named them like that so it would go with Brad and Alissa. *B* and *A*. Brad and Alissa. Beth and Ami."

"No, they didn't," Anna said. "Their mother gave them American names because she hoped they would be adopted by an American, isn't that right, Dad?"

"That's what Brad said."

"Why didn't their mother want them?" Mallory asked.

Steven looked in the rearview mirror. "I'm sure she wanted them. Every mother wants her babies."

"But not every mother can take care of her babies. Isn't that right, Dad?" Anna asked. "I asked Alissa, and she said that Ami and Beth's mom was only sixteen, and she wasn't married."

"That's right," Steven said.

"I heard their mom died," Mallory said.

"She was in the hospital for a long time," Anna said. "And then she died."

"I feel so sorry for Beth and Ami," Mallory said. "I mean, I'm happy that they're being adopted by Brad and Alissa. I'm just sorry for them that their lives have been so hard and they're so little. The good thing is that now they're going to have a mom and a dad who really love them. I wish everybody could grow up with both a mom and a dad who love them."

Steven reached over and covered Genevieve's hand with his and gave it a squeeze. A very small corner of her stone-cold heart chipped off. Maybe a lot of things weren't good in her marriage, but Genevieve knew it was good she and

Steven were still together. He was a wonderful father, and she tried to be a good mother. At least their daughters had the advantage of growing up with two parents who loved them.

"You know what I read in a magazine?" Anna added, as their car pulled into the church parking lot. "I read that it's not as important for a child to know that her parents love her as it's important for a child to know that her parents love each other."

Genevieve tried not to flinch. Anna, their smart, sensitive, intuitive daughter didn't miss a thing. Her words seemed to seep into Genevieve's tightening shoulder muscle and give it a pinch, sending a shooting pain up her neck and straight out her left eyebrow.

The last thing in the world Genevieve wanted to do right now was enter a sanctuary full of smiling faces and sit in a pew between her perceptive fourteen-year-old daughter and her unruffled husband.

What has happened to me? Four years ago this moment would have been everything I prayed for. Why has my life turned inside out? All my nerves are on the outside of my skin. And to think that a month ago I thought God was going to make me well. I've only gotten worse.

Chapter Nine

Glenbrooke Community Church's doors were doubled up with greeters. Genevieve had an aversion to greeters. She didn't like people welcoming her when she didn't want to be there in the first place. Their openness diametrically opposed her closeness. Four people shook Genevieve's hand before she and her brood made it into a middle pew on the left side.

She sat down and stared at the bulletin that had been handed to her so she wouldn't have to make eye contact with anyone sitting near her. Everything felt different from when she had been here last. The bulletin's format was different. The new cushions on the pews were different.

She cautiously peered up and felt a sense of relief that the front of the church was as she remembered. The church's original stained glass window was nearly 120 years old. It had been designed and cut on the East Coast, brought overland on the Oregon Trail, and pieced together when it arrived in Glenbrooke. The image in the window was of Christ the Good Shepherd. He held a lost lamb in His arms and was gazing at it tenderly.

Genevieve felt a specific sort of hope seeing something beautiful that had been made from so many shards of broken glass. Her task, several weeks ago, of removing all the bits of glass from the flowerboxes in front of the café windows had taken her several hours, but all those pieces had been thrown away.

Someone told Genevieve when she had first attended the church and had commented on the window that two of the glass pieces that made up the lamb Jesus held in His arms had come from Georgia. They were two of only a dozen pieces of glass that survived a Civil War battle that severely damaged the church outside of Atlanta.

Setting her focus on the window, as the early summer light came streaming through, Genevieve felt a small measure of comfort despite her still racing heart. She guessed the painkillers hadn't taken over yet because not only was her shoulder still tight but her head was also pounding.

She read the words on the front of bulletin for the third time:

"But you desire honesty from the heart, so you can teach me to be wise in my inmost being" (Psalm 51:6, NLT).

Mallory readjusted her position, scooting closer to Genevieve and whispering, "I don't see Beth and Ami."

Genevieve pressed a finger to her lips, and Mallory continued to look around the sanctuary.

The nervousness grew inside Genevieve until her stomach gurgled a loud protest to all the acid she was sending down. It was more acid than her stomach needed to work on the two painkillers, glass of grape juice, and slice of wheat toast she had fed it for breakfast.

The congregation was invited to stand and sing at the beginning of the service. Genevieve was surprised to find that the only accompaniment was a piano and the song came from a hymnbook. The last time she had been here, a white screen had come down in front, covering the stained glass window. Words to lively choruses that Genevieve didn't know were projected on the screen as a group of instrumentalists, two young men and one rather expressive young woman, led the congregation in singing the songs.

It had impressed Genevieve as being a lively way to sing but a departure from what she had anticipated from an old, traditional church. She liked singing this morning with her head down and her gaze lost in the words in the hymnbook she held. The hymn was entitled, "Lord, Open Thou My Heart to Hear," and Genevieve noticed in the upper right-hand corner that the song had been written in Wittenberg, Germany, in 1543. She felt comforted to have a small reminder of the Old World. She had never heard the song before, but she sang aloud as if she had.

Lord, open Thou my heart to hear
And through Thy Word to me draw near
Let me Thy Word e'er pure retain
Let me Thy child and heir remain.

The simplicity of that first verse brought Genevieve a spark of guilt. She knew her heart wasn't open. It hadn't been for a long time. She only read the second verse silently as the others sang it. Long ago her father had taught her never to say anything unless she meant it. He had drilled in her that that principle applied to songs, creeds, and vows as well. She couldn't sing the second verse with the others because she knew the words didn't line up with what she was experiencing in her life.

> Thy Word doth deeply move the heart,
> Thy Word doth perfect health impart
> Thy Word my soul and joy doth bless
> Thy Word brings peace and happiness.

The hymnbooks closed, and a prayer was given from the pulpit. Then the congregation was invited to sing a contemporary song before sitting down. The words were printed on the back of the bulletin. She was surprised to see that Mallory and Anna knew the song by heart and sang cheerfully.

The tune was lighthearted, and the words were about loving Jesus and walking closely with Him every day.

Genevieve glanced at Steven. He seemed to be taking it all in. Genevieve had a feeling he would like the combination of old hymns and new choruses, even though he didn't sing along with either. Steven liked fairness and equality. He would notice that this church was trying to offer something for every age.

When the new pastor, Gordon Allistar, stepped behind the pulpit, all eyes were up front. His Australian accent seemed to draw the congregation into his message since hearing such an accent in Glenbrooke was a novelty. He wore a respectable looking suit and appeared well enough informed. Something was engagingly fresh about his preaching style. He just spoke. He spoke as if he were talking to one person instead of several hundred.

Mallory leaned against Genevieve during the message and twisted Genevieve's gold bracelet around and around her wrist. Steven appeared attentive, and Anna kept glancing between both parents as if checking to see if they were listening to everything the pastor was saying. It occurred to Genevieve that anyone who looked at the Ahrens family would think they were the model Christian family. How could anyone suspect that this was Steven's first visit to church and the last place Genevieve wanted to be?

At the end of the service, the pastor asked Alissa and Brad to come up front with their daughters, Beth and Ami. Genevieve smiled when she saw the proud look on Brad's clean-shaven face and the joy on Alissa's beautiful face. They each held one of their daughters. The girls were shyly holding on to their new parents and looking away from the crowd.

Pastor Allistar spoke directly to each of the little girls, making eye contact with them and gently patting their shoulders. "You are a precious gift," he said, even though the girls didn't understand English yet. "We are all so glad you're here. As a church family, we promise to care for you and be

WILDFLOWERS

here for you as you grow. It's my prayer that as a church, we can demonstrate to you that God loves you and cares for you. He is the one who brought you here. He is the only one who will always be there for you no matter what."

One of the girls, the one Alissa was holding, seemed to be carefully listening to the pastor. As soon as he said, "He is the only one who will always be there for you," the little girl held out her arms to Pastor Allistar as if she wanted him to take her in his arms.

The congregation gave a quiet "ohh" in unison, as she went to him and nestled her head against his shoulder. Pastor Gordon gazed at the little one in his arms. He stood directly under the stained glass window. Streams of color-infused light poured over the shepherd of this small church as he held this little lamb in his arms. The harmony between the living moment and the art frozen in colored glass was stunning.

Genevieve glanced at Steven. His mouth had opened in a tiny *O*, turning his face into a charming exclamation point.

Everyone spoke of that glowing moment afterwards at the luncheon held in the church's multipurpose room. They all saw the symbolic imagery. Steven said on the way home that the whole church experience had been different than what he had expected and much more enjoyable. Anna seemed pleased with his evaluation.

Genevieve remained quiet. She had been holding so much in for so long it wasn't hard to keep her thoughts and feelings to herself.

Tuesday morning, Steven left for a fifteen-day stretch.

That night, when Genevieve went to bed, she missed him. For so many years she had steeled herself against feeling any sense of loss when he left town that it made her mad to feel this loneliness all over again.

All night long she tossed and wrestled. The words from Sunday's hymn kept running through her mind.

Thy Word doth deeply move the heart,

Thy Word doth perfect health impart.

She shot long questions heavenward, not quite willing to label them as prayers, yet knowing this was the most she had conversed with God in a long time.

When none of her questions received any hint of an answer, she turned on the light and went downstairs, looking for her Bible. She found it, after a search, and sat in the living room at two in the morning, with no idea where she should start to read.

What part of God's Word will move my heart? Which verses will bring me health?

All she could remember was that the women in the Bible study that had met at the Wildflower Café were reading in John. Genevieve turned to the book of John. She read three chapters and felt comforted. Her heart didn't feel particularly moved, nor did she feel a surge of improved mental health. But then she realized she wasn't reading in a way to study and ponder deeper meanings. She was just reading. Observing instead of absorbing.

Sometime around four in the morning, Genevieve felt chilled and realized that she had fallen asleep on the couch. She returned to bed and slept solidly for a few hours before getting up to take the girls to school.

That afternoon, Genevieve combed her hair, put on some lipstick, picked up her Bible, and marched out to her car. Gathering all her courage, she drove to Jessica's mansion on the hill. She arrived precisely at two-thirty. Walking up to the front door with her Bible under her arm, she knocked.

No one answered.

Glancing around, Genevieve realized no extra cars were parked out front. Even the golden retrievers that usually greeted guests to the Buchanan home hadn't made an appearance. The weekly Bible study must have found a different place to meet.

Genevieve hurried back to her car feeling her face flushing red. She should have called first.

Driving back into town, Genevieve decided to make a trip to the grocery store as a way of killing time before the girls got out of school. While meandering down the cereal aisle, Genevieve ran into Alissa. Ami and Beth were both sitting inside the grocery basket, wearing matching overalls and pink T-shirts.

"How are you doing?" Alissa gave Genevieve a hug. "I didn't get to talk to you much on Sunday. Brad and I appreciated you and Steven being there. It meant a lot to us."

"I'm glad we were there, too."

"What's been happening with the café? Brad said they haven't done much work yet."

"No, it's been a long process. All that's happened so far is that the builder has torn out everything that was damaged. None of the rebuilding has started. I thought someone would begin on the cabinets this week, but it looks as if they're not ready for him yet."

The older girl, Beth, squirmed in the grocery cart. She patted Alissa on the arm and spoke to her in Romanian.

"Are you ready to go home?" Alissa asked her.

"Home," Beth repeated.

Alissa smiled at her and held up her finger. "Okay. One minute."

Beth responded by holding up one finger.

"What are you doing after you finish your shopping?" Alissa asked.

"Picking up my girls and going home."

"Do you have time to come over to our place? Brad and I wanted to talk to you and Steven about something."

"He's flying this week," Genevieve said. "He won't be home until the twenty-sixth."

"Could you and the girls come by? I'd love to have the three of you stay for dinner. We're just having chicken, but we have plenty."

"You don't have to make dinner for us."

"No, I'd like to. This will be a good chance for us to talk."

"What can I bring?"

"How about a salad? And come over as soon as you're ready. Don't wait for dinnertime."

"Okay, we'll be there in about an hour."

"Good," Alissa said. "We'll see you then."

Genevieve gathered some fresh ingredients for a salad and picked up her girls from school. They were excited about the chance to see Beth and Ami.

With a large bowl of salad and two types of dressing, Genevieve and her daughters arrived at Brad and Alissa's home around four-thirty. Their small house was tucked into a glen of sheltering cedar trees. At the edge of their property in the back was a creek.

Genevieve and the girls followed the sound of voices around to the back of the house and found Brad building a playhouse for his new daughters. Beth and Ami seemed to be enjoying every minute of the construction.

"Hello!" Genevieve called out.

"Hey, glad you came over," Brad said. "Alissa is inside. How are you girls doing?"

"Fine," Anna and Mallory answered in unison.

Beth and Ami stood still, watching the older girls with huge eyes and curious expressions. It took only a few moments before each of them selected her "big sister" for the evening. Beth went to Mallory, and Ami, the littler one, went to Anna. Genevieve knew her girls would love playing the role of nanny to these sweet little ones.

Genevieve entered the back door into the kitchen where Alissa was loading the dishwasher.

"I'm so glad you guys came over," Alissa said. "I've been wanting your girls to spend time with Beth and Ami. This is perfect."

"Thanks for inviting us."

"I just put the chicken in the oven," Alissa said. "It'll be an hour before we eat. Would you like something to drink?"

"No, I'm fine. Thanks."

"I have to show you what we did with the girls' room." Alissa motioned for Genevieve to follow her down the hall.

Brad and Alissa's house had been custom built more than a decade ago. The finer touches were seen in the mantle on the wood-burning fireplace and the skylights above the entryway. The house was small and efficient with three, good-sized bedrooms. Alissa ushered Genevieve into the room they had fixed for Beth and Ami and stood in the doorway.

The twin beds were against opposite walls that were painted a pale blue. The carpet was green like grass, and all around the room were a dozen bright sunflowers painted on the walls, transforming the room into an indoor summer garden.

"This is adorable!" Genevieve said. "I didn't know you painted."

"I didn't do the painting," Alissa said. "Your daughter did. Didn't Anna tell you about painting this room?"

Genevieve tried to mask her surprise. "Anna said she helped to paint, but I thought she meant painting with rollers and brushes."

"No, we had the base coat on the walls already the night she came for the sleepover with the girls from church. Then she stayed with us for the rest of the weekend while you and Steven were at the coast."

"I remember," Genevieve said.

"Anna came up with the idea for the sunflowers on the walls when she saw the pillows I'd bought for the beds. We were going to paint just one big sunflower in the corner, but once we started, we couldn't stop. Beth and Ami were so cute when we first brought them into their room. They kept touching the flowers. Ami still stands on her bed and pretends to sniff them."

"It's wonderful," Genevieve said. "I hadn't realized Anna did this. It's darling. How are you and the girls adjusting to this new life all of you suddenly have?"

Alissa leaned against the wall and smiled softly. She had on a sunny yellow T-shirt and jeans, which blended nicely with the room's décor. "I think we're doing okay. It's a big adjustment for all of us. The girls still sleep together in one bed. I don't think they quite understand that they each have their own bed. The language barrier is the biggest problem. We're noticing they've only picked up about five or six English words in the weeks they've been with us. I know it will take a while."

"I noticed at the grocery store that Beth knows the word *home*," Genevieve said.

"Yes. They both know the word *home*."

"Do they seem to understand that you're their parents now?"

"I don't know. They've been through so much. They don't have names for Brad and me yet. They just pat us on the arm when they want something. It's still sinking in for both of us that we have two daughters."

"A double blessing." Genevieve smiled. "The only thing better than two daughters is three daughters."

A wistful shadow of something painful seemed to brush across Alissa's expression. "I actually do have three daughters. I don't know if you knew I had a baby when I was a teenager. I had a baby girl."

Genevieve tried to control her surprised expression. "No, I didn't know."

"It's taken me years to get to the point I can mention it so openly. Brad has really helped me to see that Shawna was a gift from the Lord. She's almost fifteen now."

"The same age as Anna," Genevieve said.

Alissa nodded. "When I first met you in Pasadena, Anna captured my heart."

Genevieve nodded. She remembered the bond that had blossomed between Anna and Alissa. Anna was around eight at the time and always finding excuses to visit Alissa at the duplex next door.

"I wish I had been strong enough to tell you then. It would have helped you to understand why I had such a need to shower attention on Anna. I guess I thought that I could give to Anna a little bit of the love I had never been able to give to Shawna."

Lowering herself to the edge of one of the beds, Genevieve said softly, "Tell me about Shawna."

Alissa didn't sit. She stood beside the door. Her countenance remained steady and peaceful. "I had some pretty wild teenage years. By the time I was sixteen, I had lived on air force bases around the world. I think I told you that before."

"Your father was an air force pilot, wasn't he?" Genevieve asked.

Alissa nodded.

"So he was never home," Genevieve surmised.

Alissa nodded again. "I was an only child, and my mom spent more time drinking than she spent with me."

Genevieve didn't blink. She understood what it was like to be an only child. She knew what it was like to live in a pilot's home. Fortunately, she hadn't turned to alcohol in her stretches of loneliness.

"I was so full of anger." Alissa sighed. "No one knew it because it didn't show on the outside. But after my dad died, my heart was stone. I'm not sure exactly why, but my mom decided she and I should spend the summer at a beach house in southern California. She had been to Newport Beach when she was a teenager, and I guess she wanted to relive happier memories or something.

"I was seventeen that summer. When I look back now, I see that I was pretty cold, hard, and empty. Of course, at the time I didn't realize it. I met this guy on the beach. He was cute. Daring. Younger than me." Alissa shrugged. "I had nothing to lose, you know? I had no feelings left for anything or anyone. Shawn and I had a few intense days together, and then I couldn't stand the thought of him. I remember going to a party at his house one night and taking off with another guy right away because I didn't want to see Shawn."

Genevieve had never heard Alissa talk about her past this much before. She was surprised at how open Alissa was. It seemed she was different. More at peace, even with such painful memories.

"Shawn died the night of that party. He was stoned and

tried to bodysurf near the jetty. I remember feeling like this fortress I had built around my heart was beginning to crumble. For the first time, I think I was worried about what God might think of me. If I died, I was worried about what God would do with me.

"We left Newport Beach right after that. Not because of Shawn, but because my mom had gone overboard again with her drinking and became violent. I was frightened and called the police. Right after that I flew back to Boston where I moved in with my grandmother. I was living with her when I found out I was pregnant." Alissa shook her head. "If you can imagine, there I was, living with my proper Bostonian grandmother; my father was dead, my mother was in rehab, and I was carrying the child of a guy I had only spent a few days with before he died. Talk about hitting rock bottom."

"Alissa," Genevieve said sympathetically, "you've been through so much."

Alissa nodded silently. "It took a lot before God got my attention. We can be stubborn sometimes, can't we?"

Genevieve didn't answer. She clenched her teeth, determined not to show any of the stubborn bitterness she knew was stuffed down deep inside her.

"You know what?" Alissa said. "I want to show you something."

Chapter Ten

enevieve followed Alissa to the room at the end of the hallway that had been converted into an office for her Wing and a Prayer Travel Agency. Alissa seemed so calm and composed even in the midst of her incredible story. She reached for an ornately decorated wooden box on one of the bookshelves and pulled it down.

"Some of my favorite customers from Pasadena brought this box for me from Italy," Alissa said. "Do you remember my ever telling you about Chet and Rosie?"

"I'm not sure. Maybe."

"Well, they have quite a story. They are the cutest, most in-love couple I've ever known. They taught me so much about romantically loving my husband for the rest of my life. The two of them must be in their eighties now, but they still hold hands and whisper little love messages in each other's ears."

Alissa laughed. "Except the last time we saw them, they were both getting so hard of hearing that even when they thought they were whispering sweet nothings, everyone in the room could hear them."

Lifting the lid of the beautifully crafted box, Alissa removed a small stack of folded papers. "These letters changed my life. It's possible that they even saved my life. I've read them a hundred times. Especially this one." She lifted what looked like about five sheets of ordinary notebook paper that had been folded four times.

"This one is from a guy named Todd. He was one of Shawn's closest friends, and Todd was a strong Christian. Even at sixteen he had an incredible understanding about God. The other letters are from a girl named Christy. I met her on the beach the same summer I met Shawn and Todd. Christy was the first person who ever explained to me how to become a Christian. She was pretty shy in person, but in these letters she said what she felt and what she believed. These words changed everything."

"That's amazing." Part of Genevieve wanted to reach for the stack of letters, sit in a quiet corner, and read them. But they were Alissa's private letters, and she wasn't offering to share them.

"One of these letters actually prompted me to give Shawna up for adoption. I was going to try to raise her on my own, but giving her over to the couple who took her was definitely the right thing to do. I remember the day I took Shawna to the legal offices and signed the papers. The couple held her in their arms and prayed aloud, right in front of the lawyers and everyone. They thanked God for her. I wasn't a Christian yet, and I thought they were gutsy to do that. But when Brad and I went to the orphanage in Basel to get our girls, we did the same thing."

"Basel?" Genevieve asked. "I thought the girls were from Romania."

"They are. They had been transferred to a large orphanage in Basel. That's where we went to pick them up." Alissa put the box of letters back on the shelf and reached for a photo in a large frame from off her desk.

"I hadn't realized that you and Brad went to Switzerland," Genevieve said. "You knew that I grew up in Zurich, didn't you?"

"Yes, I knew that. Brad said you were from Lucerne, but I thought it was Zurich. We had a wonderful time in Basel. Short but very sweet." Alissa held up the photo for Genevieve to see. "This is what I wanted to show you."

Genevieve smiled. Alissa and Brad apparently were in a hallway at the Basel orphanage. Each of them held one of the girls while receiving a huge hug around the neck. The look of tearful joy on their faces was priceless. Whoever took the photo certainly captured just the right moment.

"This is the amazing part." Alissa pointed to something else in the photo. "After we got home and had this enlarged, I noticed we were standing right up against the wall. Do you see this picture? It was hanging on the wall, but I didn't notice it when we were there."

"It's too bad you were so close to the picture," Genevieve said. "The way you and Brad are standing, it almost looks as if the young woman in the picture is standing in between the two of you."

"Exactly," Alissa said. "But the strangest part is that the young woman in the picture looks so much like Christy, the girl I was telling you about."

Genevieve looked closely. Since the photo was so large, it was easy to see the face of the young woman on the wall. She was bent over one of the children from the orphanage who appeared to be working on some sort of embroidery or sewing. The young woman had looked up with an open-hearted expression that made it appear as if she were smiling her warm blessing on the new parents.

"That's amazing," Genevieve said. "It's angled just right, isn't it?"

Alissa nodded and took the picture back to stare at it again. "I told Brad I wanted to e-mail the Basel orphanage and ask if by any chance the young woman in the picture was named Christy Miller. It would be so fitting for her to be there at that moment, smiling on us when we got our daughters. But I didn't e-mail them because Brad kept teasing me, saying I was looking for an angel behind every bush."

Genevieve laughed. "Did your friend Christy ever go to Switzerland?"

"I have no idea. Christy and I lost contact with each other years ago."

"Did you lose contact with Todd also?"

"Yes. I always hoped the two of them would end up together." Alissa sighed and lifted her chin as she glanced out the window. "I guess I also hoped for a long time that I could redo something of my stormy past. But we can't go back, can we? After we get our hearts right with God, we can only go on and be thankful for what we have."

"And now you have two beautiful daughters." Genevieve fished for something to say. She knew that probably wasn't what Alissa meant about redoing her stormy past, but it was the first thing that came to her mind. It also kept the topic on Alissa and didn't leave room for Genevieve to think about how hard she had tried to convince herself that she and Steven couldn't go back and do anything about the lost inheritance money.

"Yes, I have two daughters in my everyday life. They are a beautiful gift from God." Alissa pressed her lips into a wobbly smile and met Genevieve's gaze. "But I will always have three daughters in my heart."

A space of silence encompassed the two women, as Genevieve tried to take in what it must have meant for Alissa to give up her firstborn daughter for someone else to raise.

As if Alissa could predict the route Genevieve's thoughts were going, she offered, "I think that something deep inside of me needed to respond to God when Brad and I found out about Beth and Ami. I needed to adopt these girls perhaps more than Brad did."

"I don't know about that. Your husband is about the most attentive, adoring father around."

"He is," Alissa agreed. "He was so ready to have kids. For me, it was more than just the longing to start a family. Maybe it's because I understood the other side of adoption. Do you know what I mean? I knew how important it was for a mother to know someone else was eager to love and care for her daughter when she wasn't able to fulfill that role. I wanted to be to Beth and Ami's mother what Shawna's adoptive mother had been to me so many years ago in that lawyer's office."

"You are amazing, Alissa." Genevieve took in the young woman standing beside her. "You have such deep understanding and such a gentleness about you. I've never seen you so at peace. These are huge issues. This is all life changing for you and Brad."

"I know," Alissa said. "God has been working in my life. I had a lot to work through. The biggest step for me was learning how to forgive from my heart."

Just then the sound of a little girl's wail was heard followed by a slamming door.

"Mom," Mallory cried out. "Mom, where are you?"

Alissa and Genevieve rushed to the kitchen. Mallory stood by the sink, running cold water over Ami's hand.

"She got a little cut on her finger," Mallory said. "She wasn't crying until she saw the blood. Then she started to wail."

"Let me see it, Ami," Alissa said.

Ami held out her small hand. Both the blood and the cut were barely visible.

"Would you like a Band-Aid?" Alissa opened the cupboard and pulled out an unopened box. "I don't think the girls saw Band-Aids like this at the orphanage. I've gone through a whole box during the past two weeks. They wear them like badges of honor or something."

Alissa wrapped the bright orange strip around Ami's index finger, and a smile came to Ami's tear-streaked face.

"Is your owie all better, Ami?" Mallory took her young charge back into her arms. "Owie, Ami? Is it gone now?"

"Owie-Ami," the little girl answered.

They all laughed.

"Yes," Alissa said, "you are my Owie-Ami. You get at least a bump or bruise a day, don't you?"

"You're not Owie-Ami," Mallory said. "Your name is Ami. What's my name? Do you remember? What's my name? Can you say, 'Ma-lo-ree'?"

"Ree," Ami said proudly. "Ree."

Mallory laughed. "Okay, you can call me Ree for now. Do you want to go back outside to swing?"

"Sing," Ami repeated. "Sing."

"Not sing. Swing. Come on, let's go swing."

"Sing," Ami said.

The two of them exited the kitchen, and Alissa reached for an oven mitt to check on the chicken. "Mallory's last day of school is tomorrow, right?"

"Yes."

"I wonder if I could hire her this summer to come over a few times a week to play with the girls and to work on their English? Ami seems to copy everything Mallory says. She doesn't do that with Brad and me."

Genevieve looked out the kitchen window and watched both her daughters playing with Alissa's little girls. "I don't think you'll have to pay either of my girls to come over here any time you want them. They both seem to enjoy having a new little sister to be with."

"I'll work something out with them." Alissa motioned toward the lemonade pitcher. "Would you mind carrying that outside along with those plastic glasses? We're just about ready to eat."

Genevieve helped Alissa set up their summer supper on the patio. The group joined hands as they stood in a circle, and Brad prayed for them. Genevieve felt herself tearing up. This was the closeness she had hoped to experience when she had moved to Glenbrooke. But instead she had closed off herself and kept too busy to be included in quiet circles like this.

The evening sky paled to a soft shade of blue as they dined together. The four girls took their plates to the child-sized picnic table beneath the fragrant evergreen trees' thick boughs. Anna's legs were too long to fit beneath the table so she pulled a wooden Adirondack chair over and presided over the girls like a garden queen.

Alissa, Brad, and Genevieve got comfortable in the padded chairs on the patio. As soon as Genevieve took a bite of Alissa's chicken, she knew she had to have the recipe.

"It's so easy," Alissa said. "It's definitely not low-calorie, but it's quick, and the girls loved it when I made it last week. Remind me, and I'll write down the recipe for you before you go home."

"You could add it to the menu at the new Wildflower Café," Brad said. "You could list as Alissa's Ritzy Chicken."

"You know," Genevieve said, "that's a good idea. It would be fun to add some more favorites from Glenbrooke residents. Good suggestion, Brad."

Brad and Alissa exchanged glances, and Brad said, "We have another suggestion for you."

"What's that?"

Brad looked at Alissa again and then said, "Would you be interested in buying our side of the building at a very reasonable price?"

Genevieve swallowed the bite of chicken in her mouth and waited for Brad to elaborate.

"We found a warehouse," Alissa said. "Have you seen the new construction on Highway 14 on the way to Edgefield?"

Genevieve nodded.

"I know the builder," Brad said. "He's putting up a string of warehouses that are also zoned for office space. I have an opportunity to expand my business, but I need more room than I had on Main Street. The warehouse would allow me to accept larger shipments of computers, plus the builder is offering me a great deal on a two-year lease."

"I see," Genevieve said slowly.

"We wanted to offer the space to you first," Alissa said. "In case you wanted to knock out the wall and expand the café."

Genevieve nodded. Inside, her imagination had begun racing like a child at an Easter egg hunt. She ran from one clump of thoughts to another, gathering ideas with glee and stuffing them all in her imagination basket. On the outside, she was trying to stay calm. It didn't seem likely that she could come up with the money, even though Collin Radcliff had pulled off the surprise of the historical site funding.

"I plan to continue my travel agency here at home," Alissa said. "I want to be here with the girls, and it's really part-time work now, anyhow."

"Ever since Lauren put in the antique store at the end of Main Street, they say more tourists have been coming to Glenbrooke," Brad said. "That could be good business for the café once it's rebuilt."

"And you did know that a bed and breakfast is going in a few blocks from the antique store, didn't you?" Alissa asked. "I was so surprised when Shelly told me at the May Day event, but she said that Jake and Meredith are buying the old Wilson house as an investment, and Meredith and Shelly's parents are moving here. They're going to run the B and B."

"Are you sure?" Genevieve asked. "The last I heard, Shelly and Meredith's father was having some kind of surgery."

"It was on his foot or knee," Alissa said. "Nothing major. He's retiring. I guess they're really excited about it. They want to call it The Hidden House Bed and Breakfast."

"I would guess that a bed and breakfast in Glenbrooke would do a real good business," Genevieve said.

Alissa nodded. "You don't have to let us know right away about buying our side of the building. I'm sure you'll want to talk about it with Steven. We're not in any hurry. We just wanted to present you with the option before you got very far with the rebuilding in case it would change things dramatically for you."

"It's like I told you at the grocery store today, the builders haven't been able to do anything yet," Genevieve said. "We've had all kinds of slowdowns and problems obtaining permits and everything else. I thought we'd be halfway through by now, but it's going to be quite a while."

"I'm sure it will go quickly once they can start," Alissa said.

"I love the idea of expanding," Genevieve said. "I'm sure you both knew that I would like the idea. But you're right about the practicality of how it would all work out. I just don't know about the finances up-front."

The three of them discussed how much Brad and Alissa had in mind for their side of the building and how the payments might be arranged. Genevieve knew they were offering it to her for lower than the actual value. True, no repairs had been made since the fire, but their side hadn't been as severely damaged. Brad's insurance policy had covered the loss of his equipment, and Brad had been working in the front part of the shop without opening it to the public.

"Take some time to think about it and pray about it," Brad said. "I'm sure Steven will have some ideas. Let us know when you decide."

For the rest of the week, Genevieve thought of little else than what she would do if the additional space could be hers. She gathered all the information logically and systematically, as if she were responsible for presenting a full report to Steven when he returned.

Genevieve let her imagination run wild, as she planned what she would do with the extra space. When the builder hit another snag after the electrician ran into delays while rewiring the kitchen, he told Genevieve it might be the end of June before he could start to rebuild the inside structure of the kitchen. She told him that was fine. She resisted the urge to tell him she might double his task. Biding her time and collecting all her information, she waited until Steven came home.

Genevieve baked a cherry cobbler for him and had a fresh pot of his coffee blend ready. The girls were over at Brad and Alissa's when Steven pulled his sports car into the garage. He had been driving with the top down and had a fresh outdoor glow on his face. Genevieve met him with a hug, a kiss, and a smile.

"What?" Steven looked around. "What's going on?"

"I have something to talk to you about." Genevieve pointed to the kitchen table, spread with papers. "Are you interested in talking now?"

"That depends," Steven said cautiously. "What is it you want to talk about?"

"The café."

"Oh." Steven put his car keys on the counter. He glanced at some of the papers. "You've been making more plans, I see."

Without sitting down or offering any of the cobbler, Genevieve dove right in and told him about the offer from Brad and Alissa. Steven's expression didn't change as she gave him a quick overview of what it would cost and how they might pull it all together.

"You're pretty excited about this," Steven observed.

Genevieve nodded.

He picked up one of the rough sketches of the floor plan from off the table. "What about booths? Do you think you might put in some booths by the windows? I always liked those booths, you know. It's relaxing to sit in a booth."

"We could consider some booths."

"What does Leah think?"

"Leah?"

"Yes, have you gone over this with Leah?"

"No."

"I thought you would discuss this with her. Don't you consider her your business partner?"

"Not really. She's a coworker. My associate. I'm sure she'll want to hear all the details, but I didn't want to tell anyone what I had in mind until I spoke with you first."

"You did?" Steven looked surprised.

"Of course. You're my partner, Steven. My business partner and financial partner."

"And?" Steven looked intently at Genevieve.

"You're my husband," she said.

Steven seemed to study her expression in an effort to discern the extent of her sincerity. "You really mean it, don't you?"

"Mean what? That you're my husband?"

"No, that you didn't go ahead with any of these plans or enlist the support of anyone else. You waited until you could talk to me."

"Yes."

"That means the world to me, Gena. I can't tell you. Thank you."

She didn't understand why that was such an issue for him or why he was taking it so seriously. "You're welcome. And by the way, I made some coffee. Cobbler, too. Are you hungry?"

The two of them sat at the kitchen table with coffee and cherry cobbler. Steven studied the papers more thoroughly and listened to Genevieve dream aloud about the café.

"What about…" Steven began.

"What?"

"This is extreme," he said. "But what about a tree house in the corner?"

"A tree house?"

Steven made a rough sketch on the floor plan. "You said you wanted to have a separate section for private meetings and you wanted to do something that would draw in more families. You could put it here, in this corner like this. See? The steps could be on the backside so you don't see them from the front. All you would need is three or four wide steps and then a flat area large enough for, say, two kid-sized tables. The sides of the tree would have netting to keep the kids from trying to jump out."

Genevieve looked at Steven.

"I don't mean a playland sort of plastic tree," he said. "Kids wouldn't play in the tree like at a fast-food restaurant. They would actually sit at their own tables and eat there. I'm thinking of a tree that looks almost real. Something artistic. Anna could explain this better than I am. The branches could keep going and lie flat against this wall." He drew a few more lines and put down the pencil. "Something like that."

Genevieve could see it. She remembered how the girls had eaten at a little picnic table under the trees at Brad and Alissa's last week. A tree house dining area for children inside the Wildflower Café would be a hit. She could see how little Beth and Ami's eyes would grow wide at such a spectacle.

"Jonathan at Camp Heather Brook is the tree house expert," she said. "I could ask him how to do it. He might even be willing to help design it."

Steven grinned. "There you go. And then you could put a small picnic table underneath the tree branches here for, I don't know…overflow when you have too many tykes dining with you."

"If we keep all of the tree and picnic table design over here in the expanded section, then we're not taking away from the cozy conversation groupings I was trying to create here."

"What about an espresso cart?" Steven asked.

"A what?"

"They have them at all the airports. A small station that serves just coffee and pastries. You would need more employees, but you could do a walk-up window here in front of what used to be the computer store. Or, you know, you could even have two restaurants separated by the current wall. You could keep the Wildflower Café pretty much as it was before and then this other side could be an ice cream shop that serves coffee as well."

Now Genevieve's mind was swimming with possibilities. She didn't want Steven to stop the flow of his creative ideas, but her imagination could only take so much. She held up her hand. "Wait! One stroke of brilliance at a time."

Steven grinned at her. He looked young. She felt old. For the first time in many months, maybe in a few years, Genevieve wanted to feel in love with her husband again.

Chapter Eleven

After a long afternoon and evening going over all the possible plans for the Wildflower Café, Genevieve was sure about only one thing. Steven supported her. In every way he was willing to do what needed to be done to make this expanded venture work. He seemed to understand even more than Genevieve that she needed to make the café a success.

Before they went to bed that night, Steven told Anna and Mallory that he would take them to church on Sunday. The girls took the news without questioning their dad. Genevieve was mystified.

Why, after all these years, does Steven want to go to church? It was actually easier when he didn't go because it made it less noticeable that I didn't go. Now I don't feel like I can stay home.

The Ahrens family sat together again in church on Sunday, and this time Genevieve talked herself into relaxing a little more. No one had grilled her on why she had been away so long. No one acted stunned to see Steven there. The atmosphere felt open and calming. She didn't need to be defensive.

Nothing in the music or the message particularly touched Genevieve this time. But she found solace once again in studying the stained glass window. The image of Christ as the shepherd, lovingly caring for His lambs, brought comfort to her.

After church, Leah and her husband, Seth, invited the Ahrens to their home for lunch. Genevieve hesitated, but Steven was all for it, so they went.

The drive to Seth and Leah's home was gorgeous on that cloudy afternoon. Late June tended to offer mixed weather in Glenbrooke. By July the summer sun made regular visits and scorched all the wildflowers in its wake, but today the wildflowers filled the sides of the highway with streamers of brilliant color. The blues and yellows were especially vibrant as Steven drove the van deeper into the woodlands. Genevieve drank in the color and scolded herself for sticking so close to home when so much beauty lay only a few miles out of town.

Seth and Leah had built their house in a tranquil clearing in the midst of a spectacular wooded area, which they had inherited from Seth's uncle. A gravel road, lined with tall lupines and bouncy buttercups, led to what looked like an enchanted cottage right out of a fairy tale. The house wasn't overly cute or lined with fanciful gingerbread trim. It was built as a sturdy, log-framed woodcutter's cabin. The charm came from the trees and the way they stood guard along the property's perimeter.

"This is so pretty," Anna said, as they parked the van along the side of the house. "If I knew how to do watercolor, I'd paint this place just the way it is."

"You could do it, Anna," Steven said. "What would you need? A canvas and an easel? We can get you set up. You should explore other forms of art and painting."

Genevieve remembered when their eldest daughter had expressed interest in volleyball her freshman year of high school. Steven had researched local summer sports camps and arranged for Fina to participate in a prestigious group that used the UCLA campus during the summer. Fina was the youngest one there the first year, and Genevieve had urged Steven not to push their daughter so hard.

The encouragement turned out to be the best thing that could have happened to Fina. She excelled at volleyball. It became her sport all through high school and led to a college scholarship. Now she was spending the summer in Arizona, teaching volleyball clinics to high school girls and loving every minute of it.

It struck Genevieve that Steven had an ability to recognize another person's passion and special talents. Then, with confidence, he encouraged and prompted that person to develop those skills and dreams.

For the first time, Genevieve realized she had never encouraged or praised her husband's interest in flying. Piloting had been his passion for years, but she viewed it as her competition. The "love interest" that took her man away from her.

I've been so unfair.

"Coming?" Steven and the girls were already out of the van, and he was looking at her with questioning eyes. Genevieve was sitting there, stunned by the revelation that had come over her.

"Yes, I'm ready."

Leah opened the front door of her home and called out a welcoming hello. The front porch had two chairs that looked as if they were made from bent willow branches. Inside, the house was decorated with simple, sturdy furniture and clean colors. Seth and Leah's home reflected their earthy, no-frills sort of personalities and lifestyle.

In keeping with the simple way the couple lived, lunch was a meatless stir-fry, seasoned with fragrant Indian curry. Anna and Mallory ate mostly rice and helped themselves to oranges in the bowl in the kitchen. Steven had seconds on the stir-fry. Genevieve ate moderately. Her thoughts kept churning around in her stomach. It seemed to her that so much was missing in her marriage. They could experience such a deeper level of friendship and intimacy. She could have spent the last two decades appreciating her husband and supporting him in his endeavors. Instead, she had pulled back inch by inch over the long years, always finding something to be critical about.

The worst season of criticism had been their last five or so years in Pasadena. Ever since Genevieve had made her commitment to Christ and became a churchgoing believer, she had looked on Steven from a distance with distain. She was "saved," and he wasn't. She had tried hard to convert him, but he hadn't responded. The only answer for her seemed emotional detachment. Something in her mind had declared, "You're going to heaven and he isn't. Don't think about it."

And so she didn't. Steven's life was lived out at thirty thousand feet soaring above the clouds. Her life was at sea level, viewing the clouds as a sheer veil through which she would pass one day on her way to eternity.

Sitting in Leah's beautifully simple home, watching Leah interact with her husband as if she were still a newlywed, made Genevieve see how her heart had closed to her husband. Once her heart had shut out Steven, it became easy to shut out others, including the gentle Savior whom she had once worshiped openly.

"I have strawberries for dessert." Leah rose to clear the dishes. "Would you like them now? Or should we wait a little?"

Genevieve had lost her appetite.

"I wouldn't mind waiting a bit," Steven said.

Genevieve nodded her agreement.

"You haven't said much all through lunch, Gena. Are you okay?" Leah asked.

"I'm fine. I got a little lost in my thoughts."

"Thoughts about the café?" Leah ventured. "I've been wondering how things are coming along. I haven't stopped by because this was my last week working at the hospital."

"Do you have another temporary position lined up?" Steven asked.

"No, I thought I'd volunteer to do Meals for Seniors for a while and take food around to the elderly people who use that service. I know it's going to take some time till the café is up and running."

"It may be even longer than we thought." Genevieve glanced at Steven. "Brad and Alissa asked if I wanted to buy their side of the building. He's moving his company."

Leah's eyes opened wide. "Really? Oh, Gena, what a golden opportunity."

"That's what we thought," Steven said.

"Are you going to do it? Are you going to buy their side? Just think of all the ways you could expand the café!"

"I know," Genevieve said. "The possibilities are exciting. Steven and I are figuring out creative ways to come up with the funding."

Seth turned to Leah and gave her a look Genevieve didn't understand. The two of them seemed to know something Genevieve didn't.

Leah nodded at Seth. "What do you think, Seth?"

"I think this is it."

"This is what?" Genevieve said.

"Seth and I have some inheritance money that just cleared all the paperwork hoops a week and a half ago. It's not a gigantic amount, but it's just sitting in the bank. Last week we started to pray about how we should invest the money, and this looks like the answer."

"But, Leah, I can't guarantee you would see a return on your investment. It's pretty risky actually. As you know, we weren't pulling in a profit before the fire. Steven and I talked about all this last night. We could expand and make the café the best it can be, but we still might be forced into bankruptcy."

"Or it could be the biggest success story to hit Glenbrooke." Leah's eyes sparked with hope. "Did you hear about the new bed and breakfast Shelly's folks are opening at the Hidden House?"

"Yes, Alissa told me."

"Glenbrooke could experience a real surge of visitors. We could become the next featured weekend getaway town in one of Richard Palmas's books."

Genevieve didn't want to entertain any thoughts about the green-eyed gentleman who had challenged her to dazzle him when he returned to Glenbrooke.

"How would the people here feel about that?" Seth asked. "The charm of Glenbrooke is its quietness and anonymity. Would that be ruined if people flocked into town for the weekend?"

Anna jumped into the conversation. "I don't think people would flock here if there's only one bed and breakfast. This town needs the money, doesn't it? I heard people talking about how they didn't want the Wildflower to close for good because it would mean the town was beginning to die."

Steven looked at his daughter with admiration. "What do you think Glenbrooke needs, Anna?"

She hesitated, looking at the adults as if to make sure she had group permission.

Mallory, however, didn't wait for an invitation to share her opinion. "We need an old-fashioned place. Like a candy store or an ice cream parlor. If people think it's just like it used to be in the olden days, they'll come and bring their kids."

"I was going to say we need an art gallery," Anna said quietly.

"When I was a girl," Leah said, "we used to have a big weekend event called Glenbrooke Days. They closed off Main Street and had a parade in the morning. My oldest sister was the queen of the parade or whatever they called it the last year they had Glenbrooke Days."

"Did they have booths and sell crafts?" Anna asked. "Because my teacher was telling us something about how they used to do that. She has a picture on the wall next to the flag that she said she bought at a street fair in Glenbrooke when she was a teenager."

"Yes, they had booths," Leah said. "I don't remember the arts and crafts part, but I do remember the food. Somebody used to make fudge every year, and it would sell out. So my job was to stand in line and buy half a pound of caramel fudge for my dad before it was all gone."

"I love fudge!" Mallory said.

Leah chuckled. "So did my dad. He couldn't stand in line because he was in charge of the log-splitting contest. You know what? A lot of the older men who come to the café every morning for their coffee competed in that event. My favorite part was when my dad would blow the whistle, and we would all stand back as the axes were swung and the wood chips started to fly. I loved the way the air filled with the scent of cedar."

"Do you know what I think?" Steven pushed back his chair from the table and looked at the others gathered around their close circle. "It sounds like it's time to bring back the good ol' days. A Glenbrooke Days weekend would be a grand event around here, wouldn't it?"

Everyone started to talk at once, expressing agreement and questions. Seth's voice carried over the rest of theirs. "Why did they discontinue Glenbrooke Days?"

"I'm not sure," Leah said. "My guess is so many people were leaving Glenbrooke they lost their steering committee. When the logging industry cut back here, a lot of people moved to Edgefield. Glenbrooke is a different sort of town from what it was twenty years ago."

"I would help with the street fair," Anna said. "Mallory and I could do face painting like we did at that soccer tournament in Pasadena. So many little kids live in Glenbrooke now, and they would love a street fair."

"Yeah," Mallory piped up. "We could sell balloons and cotton candy, and Mom, you could make the fudge!"

Genevieve was beginning to feel more enthusiastic about the idea. She had a great fudge recipe. "We need a little more than balloons and fudge to have Glenbrooke Days, though."

"Think what it would mean to the older Glenbrooke residents," Steven said. "News of the return of the ol' Glenbrooke Days would certainly light a spark under a few of those logging legends."

"Our high school even has a marching band again," Leah said. "They disbanded it when I was in ninth grade. Wouldn't that make for a fun parade?"

"Could we have a clown?" Mallory asked. "Did you used to have a clown? Because I think Beth and Ami would love to see a real clown."

"How about it, Seth?" Leah turned to her husband and gave him a charming wink. "Would you like to be the clown?"

"I think Steven was hoping you would ask him." Seth gave Steven a nod.

"Unfortunately, I'll be flying that weekend," Steven said quickly.

"You don't even know what weekend it's going to be!" Leah laughed.

"Doesn't matter. Whatever weekend it falls on, I'll be working that weekend."

Up until Steven said that, Genevieve had been dreaming along with the others. His comment sent her spiraling down into a familiar darkness. Steven was great at making suggestions about starting up Glenbrooke Days or about Genevieve's expanding her café. But when it came down to it, he was never there to execute the plan.

For the rest of the day, Genevieve battled gut-wrenching anger and frustration toward Steven. By evening, she had slipped back into her well-rehearsed role, maneuvering through their marriage with politeness and quiet disdain.

It didn't matter that she was on the brink of partnering with Leah and expanding the café beyond her original hopes and aspirations. It didn't matter that their two families had pretty much reinvented a glorious Glenbrooke Days celebration early that fall.

All that mattered to Genevieve was that for Steven it was all talk. He wouldn't be there, most likely, for the execution of either event. He might have said it as a joke so he wouldn't have to dress up as a clown, but his track record was the same whether he was joking or not.

Feeling heaviness on her shoulders, Genevieve went to bed early.

She woke sometime in the middle of the night breathing deeply and fully aware that she had just stepped out of her reoccurring dream yet another time. She could hear the phone ringing at the Wildflower Café in the hollow chamber of her dream. Her subconscious told her Steven was calling. The grand opening would have to wait while she answered the phone.

Blinking in the darkness and hearing Steven's steady breathing beside her, Genevieve turned a dangerous corner in her mind. She completed her dream in her waking realm by picturing herself stomping over to the phone on the café's wall. She picked up the phone and yelled into the receiver, "I don't need you! I can do this without you so don't bother to come at all because I can't afford to care anymore!"

With a jerk of her arm, Genevieve visualized herself hanging up the phone and marching to the café's front door. She was determined to open that door and let the guests in despite Steven's not coming.

Even though her dream was really a conscious thought and she was planning each step rather than dreaming it, something unexpected happened. In her imagination, she couldn't open the door. It was locked. Dozens of friendly, waving people were wanting to come in, but she didn't have the key.

Chapter Twelve

hat went well, don't you think?" Alissa said before getting into her car. Her blond hair rolled over the shoulders of her light turquoise, sleeveless dress.

It was Wednesday in the early afternoon, and Genevieve and Alissa, along with Leah, were just leaving Collin Radcliffe's law offices. The three women had met to sign the legal papers documenting the sale of Brad and Alissa's office to Genevieve and Leah.

"It was quicker and easier than I thought it would be." Leah wore a dark skirt and matching blazer, which was the most professional looking outfit Genevieve had seen her in.

Genevieve had also worn one of her classiest outfits for the important meeting. Her short linen skirt and matching top were pale yellow. Around her neck she artfully had tied one of her favorite silk scarves. The light brown background of the scarf was accented with swirls of pale yellows and blues. That morning Anna had said the scarf's brown matched Genevieve's hair and the blue brought out her eyes.

"You have brown-sugar hair," Anna had commented to her mom. "I think you should highlight it this summer, Mom. It would make you look younger." Anna also advised Genevieve to use more eyeliner and a darker shade of mascara. "You really are pretty. I think Dad would notice if you would do a few little things to make yourself even prettier for him."

Genevieve tried her daughter's suggestion and spent a little more time on her eye makeup before the meeting. She also left her hair down instead of pulling it back in a clip, the way she did every day when she was working. Her thick, brown, natural wavy hair skimmed her shoulders, and when she had arrived at the meeting, both Leah and Alissa commented on how great she looked.

"What are your plans for the rest of the day?" Alissa asked Leah and Genevieve.

"I'm open," Genevieve said. As soon as she said "open" she thought of how long it had been since she had described anything in her life with that term. She felt an uncertainty come over her as she wondered what Alissa wanted.

"How about if the three of us go somewhere for lunch to celebrate this occasion?" Alissa asked. "Since Brad is home with my girls, I'm available. Where should we go?"

"I need to be at Jessica's by two-thirty," Leah said. "That doesn't leave much time for lunch unless it's someplace close."

"You know," Alissa said, "this is exactly why we need to make all the changes to the Wildflower that you suggested,

Gena. There's no place to eat around here for a special occasion. Your new café is going to revolutionize birthdays for all the women in Glenbrooke."

Genevieve laughed. "That's what I'm hoping. We could make a quick lunch at my house. I have a pasta salad already made up."

"No, we need to go out," Alissa said. "What about the country club?"

"It's so far out of the way," Leah said.

"What are our other options?" Genevieve asked. "Burgers and blizzards at Dairy Queen?"

"We could all go to Jessica's," Leah suggested.

"You mean just show up and invite ourselves for lunch?" Genevieve asked. "I don't think she would appreciate that."

"Actually, knowing Jessica, she would love it," Alissa said. "Her front porch is the perfect location for a summer luncheon. Besides, it's probably the coolest place around town today. It's really warmed up."

"Are you sure Jessica wouldn't mind?" Genevieve said.

"She won't mind." Leah punched in some numbers on her cell phone. "Jessica loves having company. Hey, Jess? Hi, it's Leah. How do you feel about adding three more to your house for lunch? Alissa, Gena, and I were trying to come up with a place we could go for lunch, and your porch is our favorite option."

Leah listened to Jessica's answer and nodded at Alissa and Genevieve. "That's what I told them. Sure. I'll tell Gena to stop by her house and grab the salad. What's that? I don't know. I'll ask her."

Leah turned the phone away from her ear. "If your girls aren't doing anything, Jessica says they're welcome to come, too."

"Thanks. I'll let them know. Tell her this is really kind of her."

Leah put the phone back to her ear. "Did you hear that? Yes. Well, it's true. You are the hospitality queen of Glenbrooke, you know. Okay, I'll tell them. Alissa and I are coming right now. Do you need us to pick up anything at the store?"

Concluding her conversation, Leah closed her folding cell phone. "Jessica said to be prepared because Travis and Teri's boys have set up a lemonade stand in the driveway, and we'll be their prime clients."

Genevieve knew that Travis was Jessica's son. He would be starting first grade in the fall and was a cute, blond, precocious child who usually was followed around by an equally blond golden retriever. Genevieve didn't know the names of Teri's twin boys. She guessed they were close to Travis's age.

"Maybe I should bring Beth and Ami along," Alissa said. "Wouldn't they love to help with a lemonade stand!"

Suddenly, Genevieve didn't feel like going. The invitation to have a celebratory business lunch at the country club with Alissa and Leah was a far cry from this community picnic on Jessica's porch, complete with lemonade stand and more toddlers than adults.

When she arrived home, Genevieve considered calling Jessica and saying that something had come up and she couldn't make it. But then she remembered that they were depending on her to bring the salad. Genevieve took her potluck role seriously. She had enjoyed the neighborhood gatherings she used to host in her garden on the Fourth of July when they had lived in Pasadena. Alissa had participated in one of those garden parties. Genevieve wasn't clear what had changed so dramatically in her life that she was now eager to find excuses to avoid groups like this.

Mustering up her courage and collecting her pasta salad, Genevieve called upstairs for the girls. When she explained the invitation, both of them were eager to go.

"We better leave a note for Dad," Anna suggested.

"Where is he?"

"Playing golf," Mallory said.

"Golf? I didn't know he was going to play golf today."

"Pastor Allistar called him about an hour ago, and they just left before you got home."

Genevieve stopped in her tracks. "Your father is playing golf with the pastor?"

The girls nodded contentedly.

As they drove to Jessica's Victorian mansion on the top of Madison Hill, Genevieve tried to think through what it meant for Steven to respond to a social invitation from a pastor.

What if Pastor Allistar also invites Steven to surrender his life to the Lord? Is Steven ready to respond? If he does, what will that mean for us? For our marriage? Will I feel differently about him then? I certainly haven't been a good example to him of a loving Christian wife. I haven't even been an example of a loving wife, let alone a Christian wife. I'm just his polite wife. His partner in raising the girls. Why does Steven stay with me? Is he satisfied with the way things are? He certainly doesn't complain.

Genevieve turned up the long, steep driveway to the top of the hill where Jessica and Kyle's home sat perched like a white crown on top of a princely knoll. At the base of the wraparound front porch, in front of a large hydrangea bush exploding with colorful light blue flowers, was the cutest lemonade stand Genevieve had ever seen.

Anna giggled before getting out of the car. "Do you have any money, Mom? I want to buy a glass of lemonade."

"Me, too," Mallory said. "Look at their hats."

All three boys stood as straight as soldiers behind their folding table lemonade stand. Travis wore a tall but crumpled white chef's hat. His ears appeared to be the only thing holding up the hat.

"Look at Josiah's hat," Mallory said. "He must have brought that with him when they moved here from Hawaii." The straw hat looked as if it had been woven from palm fronds. Coming out of the side was a long, floppy wire and from the wire hung a small fish also woven from palm fronds that had now turned pale green.

"What's the other boy's name?" Genevieve asked.

"You mean Jimmy? He's the one in the fireman's hat."

"Jimmy and Josiah," Genevieve repeated, trying to remember. If their father thought to call Steven and invite him to go golfing, Genevieve thought she should at least know his children's names. "Gordon and Teri just have the two boys, right?"

"And the baby," Mallory said.

"Boy or girl?" Genevieve asked.

"A girl, Mom. You saw her on Sunday. I was holding her after church. Remember Malia? That's Hawaiian for Mary."

"Oh, right. I remember."

Anna was already out of the car and on her way to the lemonade stand. Mallory was right behind her. Genevieve pulled the pasta salad out of the backseat and followed the girls to the front of the house where the three eager attendants were describing their lemonade options.

"This is the regular one made from a can out of the freezer." Travis's funny chef's hat slipped over his eyebrows. "And this one that looks kind of purple is made in the blender with raspberries. It's the best one, if you like raspberries."

"How much is it?" Mallory asked.

"This one is twenty-five cents a cup," Travis began.

"That's a quarter," Jimmy added.

"They know." Josiah turned his head to scold his twin brother, which caused the fish on the wire attached to his hat to dip and wobble.

"But this one with the raspberries is thirty-five cents because it cost-id more," Travis concluded his sales pitch.

"I'll have the raspberry one," Anna said.

"Me, too," Mallory said.

"You can make that three glasses of raspberry," Genevieve said.

"They aren't really glasses." Travis picked up one of the red, plastic cups. "Cuz my mom said we had to use the plastic ones."

"That's fine," Genevieve said. "We all like red, plastic cups."

"I like the blue ones," Jimmy said.

"We don't have any blue ones," Josiah corrected, giving him a nudge.

"We used to have blue ones where we used to live," Jimmy said.

Genevieve thought she had never seen a more adorable trio of young entrepreneurs. Even her three girls hadn't been as precise and industrious with their early business ventures. She found it especially admirable that these three were set up for business in the driveway of their isolated house where the clientele would be safely monitored, albeit limited. Just because they didn't live on the corner of a busy street didn't deter them from setting up shop.

"How many ice cubes would you like?" Travis carefully extracted a cube from a fancy ice bucket with a pair of tongs. The ice cube popped out of his pinch and flew to the ground.

"That's okay," Josiah said quickly. "That happens sometimes. That's why we have more ice. They just melt on the floor, and it's okay."

Genevieve suppressed her smile.

"I would like two ice cubes," Mallory said politely.

"So would I," Anna agreed.

"Two would be fine for me as well," Genevieve added.

With great effort, all three hat-wearing businessmen delivered the goods to their thirsty customers. Fortunately, the raspberry lemonade was very good, which made it easier to praise them.

"Here's two dollars," Genevieve said. "Keep the change."

"It doesn't cost-id two dollars," Travis said. "It only cost-id…"

"Thirty-five cents," Josiah said.

"Thirty-five and thirty-five and thirty-five," Travis declared.

"That would be ninety-five cents," Mallory said.

"No, it wouldn't," Anna corrected her. "It's one dollar and five cents. But you guys can keep the extra money. It's a tip."

The three boys looked at each other.

"I don't know if we're allowed to have a tip," Josiah said.

Anna and Mallory laughed. "I'm sure it's okay with your moms. A tip means you're given a little extra for doing a good job."

The boys beamed.

"Thank you!" they said in a trio of echoes.

"You're welcome," Anna said. "Thank you for the delicious lemonade."

Genevieve thought about Mallory's observation at dinner on Sunday that what Glenbrooke needed was an old-fashioned ice cream shop. There certainly was some merit to that. She wasn't sure how that could be incorporated into the Wildflower Café, but the nostalgia of a lemonade stand and an ice cream parlor was appealing. Especially on a warm, sunny day like today.

Maybe it should be a walk-up ice cream window that doubles as an espresso window in the winter. We can't put in a drive-up window, but maybe people would like a walk-up window.

Genevieve was mulling over her thoughts as she walked up the steps to the wide front porch. The day immediately felt cooler and more fragrant as she stood beside the hanging planters of large, lavender petunias.

The screen to the front door opened, and Jessica welcomed Genevieve and the girls. "I'm so glad you could come."

"I appreciate your letting us invade your afternoon like this."

"You're not invading at all," Jessica said. "The others are already here for our Wednesday afternoon Bible study. We planned last week to have a salad luncheon today. So this is perfect. I've been hoping for a long time that you could join us."

Genevieve felt trapped. Had Leah tricked her into coming to the Bible study? Genevieve discounted that just a few weeks ago she had come to this front door on her own, with her Bible under her arm, searching for the support and encouragement that was now being offered to her.

"I, ah…I may need to leave early. I'm not sure if the girls need to get home soon or not."

"Then stay as long as you can. You know you're always welcome."

"Yes," Genevieve said. "Thank you. I appreciate it, Jessica."

"Is that Gena and the girls?" Alissa's voice called from the back of the house.

"Are Beth and Ami here?" Mallory asked.

"Yes," Jessica said. "They'll be happy to see the two of you.

Ami was a puddle of tears when they arrived a little while ago. I think she was frightened of the boys because of their funny hats."

"Ami?" Mallory called out, heading to the back of the house in search of her favorite toddler. "Where's my Ami girl?"

"Ree! Ree!" came the cry before the sound of bare feet padding on the wood floor. Ami was followed by Jessica's four-year-old daughter, Emma, who was herding Ami through the dining room, as if she were a little lamb.

"Do you want Mallory and me to keep all the kids in the backyard while you have your Bible study?" Anna asked.

Jessica's soft face took on a relieved expression. "That would be wonderful. We'll all be happy to pay you for the time you spend babysitting the children."

"That's okay. We like your kids. And you have a huge backyard with lots to do. It will be fun."

"Anna, you're a sweetheart," Jessica said. "But we'll still pay you. Please make yourselves at home, and let me know if I can get you anything."

"I don't have a serving spoon for the pasta salad," Genevieve said.

"No problem. Bring it in the kitchen. I have everything set up."

Genevieve followed Jessica into the spacious kitchen where half a dozen women were standing around the counter visiting. Genevieve recognized all the women, but she didn't know everyone's name.

"You know Leah and Alissa and Lauren, of course,"

Jessica said. "And Teri and Shelly. Have you met Meredith before? Meri is Shelly's sister."

"We met at the May Day event at camp a year ago." Meredith held a sleeping baby in her arms. "Only this little guy was in my belly then instead of in my arms."

"He's so sweet," Genevieve said. "What's his name?"

"Grant. Grant Jacob."

"Strong name," Genevieve said.

"He's a strong little man already. He's only nine months old, but these overalls are size 2T."

Genevieve glanced at Meredith's sister, Shelly. Genevieve knew that Shelly and Jonathan loved their full and busy life at Camp Heather Brook, but they had let a few close friends know that they had been trying for some time to get pregnant without success. Genevieve wondered how Shelly felt standing there listening to her younger sister talk about her strong, healthy son. If Shelly was struggling with jealousy, her face showed no evidence of it.

"How long will you be here?" Alissa asked.

"Just a few more days. My parents are settling into their new bed and breakfast. Shelly thought we should all be together so our family could have a blessing party for them."

"What's a blessing party?" Alissa asked.

"Our family got together at the Hidden House last night and ate pizza. Then, because the carpet is all ripped up, we went around the house with permanent markers and wrote blessings on the old flooring. We listed the fruit of the Spirit on each of the steps and wrote verses in the middle of the floor of each of the guest rooms."

"That is so creative," Lauren said. "I'll have to remember to tell Kenton."

Genevieve would have thought Lauren would be appalled at the thought of writing on anything old with permanent markers. Lauren's antique store at the end of Main Street was filled with old furniture she had gathered from garage sales.

Lauren explained her thought. "Kenton is eager to pull off the wallpaper in our family room and replace it with wood paneling. He would love the idea of writing blessings on the wall before we put up the paneling."

Just then three-year-old Beth, who had been patiently patting Alissa's arm, said in a clear voice, "Mama."

Everyone stopped.

"Yes, Beth?" Alissa leaned down to give the girl her full attention.

"Up." Beth lifted her arms, and Alissa scooped her up.

Genevieve noticed tears in Alissa's eyes as Alissa whispered, "That's the first time she's called me Mama."

All the women gave a collective "oh!" and murmured expressions of happiness at this breakthrough for Alissa and her daughter.

Genevieve thought of the long talk she and Alissa had in Alissa's office. She remembered the way Alissa said she had learned to forgive before she could go on and feel as free as she did now. It certainly showed. In all the years Genevieve had known Alissa, she had never seen her this content and settled.

"Why don't we have a prayer together," Jessica suggested

softly. "Then everyone please help yourself to the food here on the counter, and we'll sit at the dining room table. Oh, and for the vegetarians, there are two taco salads. The one in the blue bowl doesn't have meat."

Jessica held out her hands, inviting the women to join her in a circle of prayer.

For Genevieve, something powerful and precious occurred when she held Anna's hand and listened to Jessica pray for the women in the group. Jessica went around the circle and prayed for each of them by name as well as their spouses and each of their children. Genevieve hadn't realized how many people this group represented.

As Jessica was concluding her prayer for Meredith, the last woman in the circle, the sound of a baby crying in the other room broke the solemnity of their prayer time. Jessica ended with, "And bless baby Malia, who probably wants to eat now, too. Amen."

Teri slipped out of the circle. The others began to chat as they reached for plates and helped themselves to the abundance of salads on the counter.

"Would you like me to make some lunch for the little kids?" Anna asked.

"All of them ate before you got here," Jessica said. "Except maybe Molly Sue. Lauren, did Molly eat something yet?"

"Yes, she's fine."

Teri entered with her baby girl on one hip and a baby boy on the other hip. "Lauren, guess who wasn't sleeping?"

"Michael," Lauren said, "were you keeping Malia

awake?" The round-faced little fellow cooed when he saw his mom.

Genevieve felt overwhelmed being in the midst of this overactive baby factory. She began to reconsider her idea of building a tree house inside the restaurant. If they attracted this many toddlers on an average afternoon, it would take a separate employee just to corral the troops while the moms tried to talk. She thought she might be better off turning the old storage shed into a playhouse and sending all the children out back while the adults ate.

"Anna," Genevieve whispered, "are you sure you don't mind watching all these children this afternoon?"

"I don't mind."

"Good for you. You're a braver woman than I."

Genevieve stood back as the others dished up their salads. She glanced at the wall behind her and noticed a small, framed picture next to the refrigerator. It looked like the front of an antique greeting card with gold-lettered, fancy script. Genevieve stepped closer to read the quote.

A single wildflower, given with love
Is better than
A dozen perfect roses
Given with indifference.

ANONYMOUS

The room seemed to grow quiet for Genevieve. It didn't matter that the children and babies outnumbered the adults or that the dogs had begun to bark in the backyard. She loved how the picture used a single wildflower in such a simple way. Examining the framed picture again, she thought how she might use the image or the poem at the Wildflower Café.

But then, to her surprise, her thoughts flooded with images of Steven. Unannounced, a clear, powerful realization hit her full force. Not a realization about the café, which usually dominated her thoughts, but a realization about her marriage.

For years I've been striving to present my husband with a dozen perfect roses, haven't I? I've tried to make our life together the best it can be. I feel like everything is up to me, and I work to make things perfect.

But my heart hasn't been in any of it. I'm not in love with Steven.

A fear came over Genevieve. Her weary spirit had been found out once again. She felt as if she were inwardly dashing from her previously safe, dark hiding place to find a new place to hide where she wouldn't be found out.

She looked over at the women gathered in this house. If there was ever an opportune time for Genevieve to come out of hiding and step into the light, it would be this afternoon, with these women.

Her instincts shouted, "Run! Hide! Flee back into the shadows where you know it's safe!"

But her spirit was drawn to the light. Almost as if someone were calling her by name.

Chapter Thirteen

For the first twenty minutes of the afternoon Bible study, Genevieve didn't say a word. She ate her salads and listened to the women talk. Their discussion revolved mostly around their children. They exchanged advice and hopped up whenever one of their little ones came in looking for his or her mom.

Genevieve knew she could make an excuse and leave at any time, but Anna already had collected the children who wanted to go with her and led them out of the dining room. Genevieve knew the women were appreciative of Anna and Mallory's watching the children. If Genevieve left, it would cause a noticeable gap in the afternoon plans for the others.

Keeping her thoughts to herself and trying to push aside her feelings of panic, Genevieve stayed glued to her chair at the end of the dining room table. Jessica gathered up all the empty plates, and Teri helped her to clear the table. The women pulled out their Bibles, and Genevieve noticed that each of them had a notebook and a pen ready. She had only her paper napkin in her lap. Under the table she was tearing it into tiny shreds.

"I have a few extra Bibles here." Jessica placed them in the center of the table. Meredith reached for one first, and then Genevieve took the one with the brown leather cover. It appeared to be a well-read Bible with lots of handwritten notes in the margins.

"We've been going through the book of John," Jessica said. "We're on the second half of chapter 11 this week. This is where Lazarus has died, and Mary and Martha cried to Jesus, 'If only you had been here, this wouldn't have happened.' Last week we were talking about all the times we've said that to Jesus."

Genevieve found the chapter and nodded. She knew all about feeling disappointed when the man in your life doesn't come when you want him to.

Jessica went on. "I have one more thought to add to this part of the chapter before we look at the upcoming verses. Do you remember last week when someone commented on how Jesus told the women to roll away the stone, but Mary and Martha argued with the Lord and told him that Lazarus had been dead for four days and stunk?"

One of the women chuckled.

"I looked up something from the next part when Jesus brings Lazarus back to life. He again tells the women to do something. He says, 'Unbind him, and let him go.'"

Genevieve looked down and found the verse Jessica was

referring to. It was verse 44.

"I don't know why, but I really got into this," Jessica said. "I even looked up the original word for 'unbind.' The Greek word is *aphiemi*. It also means to untie, to forgive, or to let go. The other place this same word is used is in Luke 23:34."

Genevieve had no idea these women put so much research time into their study. She thought they would discuss what the passages meant to them, the way they had that one afternoon at the café.

"You don't have to turn to the reference in Luke," Jessica said. "You'll recognize it when I tell you what it says. It's when Christ was hanging on the cross. He used the same word when He said, 'Father, forgive them.' Or unbind them, untie them. 'They don't know what they're doing.'"

Genevieve noticed that Jessica's voice had become shaky. "This was a huge revelation to me because, as most of you know, I have a relationship in my life that's basically dead to me. My father and I haven't spoken to each other in years. I dug into this passage because I felt as if my father was dead to me the way Lazarus was dead to his relatives, his sisters. I have, in a way, wrapped up my father and buried him.

"When I was studying this, I felt as if the Lord was asking me to roll away the stone that I had put in front of this relationship. Just like Mary and Martha, I argued and told God that the whole relationship stinks because it's been dead for so long."

Jessica reached for a napkin to wipe a tear that was trailing down her cheek. "I knew I simply should obey God instead of argue with Him. So last night, in my heart, I rolled back that stone. I opened myself up to that relationship once again. I know that if anything is going to be resurrected between my father and me, it will be a miracle that only God can perform. But at least the pathway is open now. The stone is rolled away. I have forgiven my dad, and God has made it clear I need to ask my dad to forgive me. I want to untie him and let him go."

Everyone around the table was quiet. The one baby in the room was sitting contentedly on his mother's lap. All the other children were outside. The afternoon sun slipped in through the lace curtains and cast a graceful pattern of light on the open Bibles on the table.

Genevieve wondered if the other women could hear her heart pounding. She knew all about rolling thick stones in front of dark caves and closing herself off from relationships. She swallowed twice and looked at her hands. She was afraid to look at the words in front of her. God might ask her to roll away the stone in her life and open herself to Steven.

"You can see why this has been really personal for me." The tears raced down Jessica's cheeks. She seemed to be crying without making any noise. It was painfully beautiful to see her face so peaceful and vulnerable at the same time.

Genevieve knew she had never cried like that. She knew she had never been in the presence of so much light, honesty, and openness.

"What I wanted to share with all of you," Jessica said, still crying without sobbing, "is that I'm going to write a letter to my father and ask him to forgive me for running away from home so many years ago. I thought I could hide by coming to Glenbrooke, but God made it clear that—"

Before Jessica finished her sentence, Genevieve pushed away from the table. In a choked whisper she said, "Excuse me," and rose. She clutched her shredded napkin and with quiet steps left the dining room, not sure where she was going. All she knew was that she couldn't sit there another minute. She needed to be alone. To breathe. To think.

Her brisk steps led her out the front door onto the porch. The boys had abandoned their lemonade stand and joined the happy noises of the other children playing in the backyard. Genevieve lowered herself onto the porch swing's padded seat and drew in the fragrance of the prolific petunias spilling over the hanging baskets.

I have to forgive Steven.

She knew that thought was true and right. She needed to roll back the stone and release her husband. If a miracle were to occur in his life, it would be God's doing, not hers. She simply understood Jessica's confession and took it as her own. She couldn't hide any longer.

Genevieve was also certain that she didn't want to block God from working in her husband's life. And she had. She had nurtured, watered, and fed a thick root of bitterness against her husband for their entire married life. At this moment, it seemed to her that she had spent years wrapping Steven in strips of grave cloth. Their marriage, their love was dead to her. It stunk.

She knew she had to roll back this stone. Right now. Right here.

"Father in heaven," Genevieve began in a whisper, "I

have been so wrong. Please forgive me. Roll away the stone that I have put in front of my heart. I've closed off myself from my husband. I know that now. I've wrapped him in my anger and bitterness, and now, Father God, I want Steven to be free. I want to be free, too."

Genevieve could picture a mental list of all the offenses she held against her husband. The money he had lost in the stock market was at the top of the list. Then his being gone so much and missing the key events in her life.

The offenses were specific. Genevieve said aloud, "Father, from my heart, I want You to forgive Steven for…"

She went down her mental list, naming each offense. Her emotions inserted the strong words that she felt.

A gush of tears began. A river seemed to be released in her heart and was pouring out her eyes. For several minutes she cried and cried, barely making a sound. The tears cleansed her. Several more specific offenses came to mind, and she spoke those as well.

Then Genevieve prayed, "I was wrong to hold all this against Steven. Please forgive me, Father God. I know that when You came into my life years ago You forgave me for everything I had ever done wrong, and yet I've been unwilling to forgive my husband for these few small things. I'm so sorry. Untie me and let me go. Untie my husband and let him go."

All she had left was a whisper when she said, "Amen." God had heard. She felt free. Deeply free.

The front door's screen opened slowly, and Alissa emerged, taking tiny steps toward Genevieve. "Are you okay?" She joined Genevieve on the porch swing.

Genevieve wiped her cheeks with the useless, shredded napkin and whispered, "Yes."

Alissa wrapped her arm around Genevieve and drew her close in a hug. It seemed a little peculiar to Genevieve that this younger woman was taking her under her wing and comforting her. But then Alissa understood. She had said that evening in her home office that she had learned how to forgive others from her heart for all the painful, dark moments in her life.

Without having to explain anything to Alissa, Genevieve knew that was what had happened to her this afternoon. She had forgiven her husband from her heart. Jessica's words had broken down the roadblocks in Genevieve's stubborn head, and the truth had penetrated her heart. The bitterness was gone. So was the aching loneliness.

"I'm finally free." Genevieve pulled back from Alissa and dabbed her nose with the back of her hand.

Alissa smiled. "I know what that feels like. It's incredible, isn't it?"

Genevieve nodded. "I can't believe it took me so long to finally get it."

"I know," Alissa said. "I was the same way. Unforgiveness is such a private thing, but it chokes us."

Genevieve nodded. She felt exhausted and exhilarated at the same time. She knew it would be awkward to return to the group. Yet she knew she needed to say something.

Alissa went inside with her. All the women greeted her with sympathetic, concerned looks.

This was a safe place to be.

Genevieve opened up and shared her heart. She felt as if the great, choking vine that had darkened her life and caused her to board up the windows of her soul was now gone. Her heart was like a cottage flooded with light and ready to welcome visitors. Forgiveness was the key that had been missing in her half-conscious, half-dreaming image of trying to unlock the café's front door.

Genevieve heard herself laughing, as she spilled out her story at the table to these understanding women. "I listened in on one of your Bible studies at the café weeks ago. You were talking about the man who gave excuses when Jesus asked him if he wanted to be made well."

"I remember," Teri said. "He had the same infirmity, whatever it was, for thirty-eight years. And Jesus healed him."

"I know what it's like to have the same problem for a very long time." Genevieve told the group about how she thought she had heard the Lord calling her by name that night by the bathtub and how He had asked her if she wanted to be made well.

"That was the night the café caught on fire," Genevieve said. "I thought for sure God hadn't heard my prayer or that it was too late for me. Why else would God allow my dream café to be destroyed right after I said I wanted my life to be better?"

A soft, knowing smile came over Jessica's face. "I think all of us have seen something like that happen in our lives. God sometimes has to tear down something before He can rebuild it the way He wants it to be built."

"You know what I was just thinking?" Lauren added. "What you've just told us, Genevieve, is exactly what this part of John 11 is all about. Weeks ago you asked Jesus to heal you, and it seemed that He didn't do anything. That's just like Mary and Martha, who asked Jesus to come while Lazarus was sick, but the Lord didn't come. Remember how they said, 'If you had been here, our brother wouldn't have died'?"

Several of the women glanced down at their open Bibles.

Shelly spoke up. "That's so true, Lauren. Jesus brought about a greater miracle by raising Lazarus from the dead than if He had come earlier and healed him before he died."

"I don't know that any miracle is greater or lesser," Shelly's sister, Meredith, commented. "But I know what you mean. We all experience different deaths in our lives. Deaths of dreams and deaths of relationships. I agree that it's pretty fabulous when a dream or a relationship you thought was destroyed comes back to life. When God brings it back to life, you know it because it's so much better than it was before."

"God is going to do something huge in your marriage, Genevieve," Alissa said. "And God is going to do something wonderful with your father, Jess. I can say that because when I settled my forgiveness issues, my heart changed so much. I'd been a Christian for a long time, but all the stuff I was holding on to from my past was keeping me bound up. I wasn't free."

"You certainly are free now." Genevieve smiled at Alissa.

"And doubly blessed," Teri added. "I know everyone said that Gordo and I were doubly blessed when we had the twins five years ago, but I look at how God provided Beth and Ami for you guys, and it's evidence of His blessings. Double blessings!"

Alissa smiled. "You know what? I have something to tell all of you. A little while ago I told Genevieve my life story, and I realized I hadn't told the rest of you what God did in my life. I've told some of you a little bit, but when I heard myself telling Genevieve my story, I realized how free God had made me."

For the next fifteen minutes, Alissa shared with the others. None of them acted stunned to learn that she had been pregnant as a teenager. All of them agreed the story was a powerful testimony to God's faithfulness. The best evidence of God's being at work in Alissa was the peace and serenity that permeated her words and her expression.

When Alissa finished, Shelly said, "Alissa, I don't know how you feel about this, but if you could come out to camp this summer and tell your story to our high school campers, I know it would be powerful. Especially the part about the letters that the teens wrote to you when you found out you were pregnant. What if those Christian teens had shunned you when you were going through the most difficult time in your life?"

"I know," Alissa said. "I don't want to think about where I would be today. God used my friends' letters in a powerful way."

"Letters can change our lives," Lauren said.

Genevieve watched Alissa give Lauren a wink and a nod. "You would know all about that, wouldn't you? If it weren't for letters, would you have fallen in love with Kenton?"

Lauren blushed slightly. "I guess God would have found another way to bring the two of us together. But I like the way He creatively chose to use letters to ignite the sparks of our love."

Teri picked up her Bible and, with a smile on her face, said, "Well said, Lauren! It's the same with God and us. He wrote this collection of love letters here in His Word to us. If He hadn't given us the Bible, I imagine He would have found another creative way to bring us to Himself. But I'm with you. I think it's blissfully romantic of God to… what did you say? Ignite the sparks of love? That's what He does with His Word. When our hearts are open to Him, He ignites all kinds of sparks as we read His love letters."

"You know what?" Jessica nearly rose from her chair. "That's what I'm going to do. I'm going to write my father a long letter. Pray for me this week, will you? You sweet ladies pray, and I'll pray, and I'll write a letter to my father."

Some of the other women said they had letters of reconciliation to write that week as well. Genevieve wondered what it would be like to write Steven a letter. They always had used the phone for any conversation they had when he was away from home. She couldn't remember ever trying to express herself to her husband in written words. The thought intrigued her.

The women left Jessica's house that day with a round of hugs and a few tender kisses on the cheek. Genevieve had never felt so surrounded with kindred souls who loved her and cared about her. She knew that her life had changed dramatically that Wednesday afternoon. She would be back the next week and the next. These women were now her lifeline.

"I wish we lived here." Meredith gave Genevieve a hug good-bye. "Do all of you know how rare it is to have such close friends and to spend time together like this?"

"We know," Jessica said. "This group is a gift from God."

Genevieve thought of all she would have missed today if she had given in to her primitive instinct to run from the light. She still would be curled up in the darkness, breathing in the stale air of her own stinking pride.

After Genevieve got in the van with Anna and Mallory to drive home, she wondered what she should say to her daughters about the changes God had made in her heart that afternoon. How much would the girls understand? How much should she say and how much should she just let them see the changes as she began to live in this new freedom?

"I've been far away from God for quite some time," Genevieve heard herself say. "A lot of things changed for me this afternoon. I just wanted you girls to know."

Her daughters were quiet for a moment. Then Anna said, "Good. I've been praying for you, Mom."

"Me, too," Mallory said.

"I've also been praying for Dad," Anna said.

"Me, too," Mallory added.

Genevieve swallowed the feelings that came with her

daughters' comments. It felt like a "glory berry" going down, full of tangy sweetness and tiny seeds of light beams that would shine inside her heart now that the door was flung wide open and ready to welcome visitors.

Steven was home when they arrived. He told them about what a good time he had golfing with Pastor Allistar, except that Gordon Allistar had a balance problem. On the third hole, Gordon missed the ball altogether on his swing and ended up toppling over. It got the two of them off to an interesting start, as Gordon filled Steven in on a long list of stories about the key moments in his life when he had lost his balance.

"He's a great guy," Steven said. "I told him I'd golf with him anytime. We might go again in a month."

Genevieve wanted to ask if they discussed anything important, like spiritual matters, but she left her questions unasked. God was doing something. She knew it now. It wasn't up to her to manipulate anything with her husband's view of Christianity like she had tried to do right after she became a Christian years ago.

Her job was to make sure she was right before God by not stockpiling any bitterness in her heart's corners, which she viewed as newly cleaned.

The first test of her resolve came the next day, when Steven reminded her that he was leaving Monday for a fourteen-day stretch.

"If I can do anything to help you on the plans for the café, we should talk about it this weekend before I leave," Steven said.

"Okay," Genevieve agreed. "And if I can do anything for you before you go or while you're gone, please let me know."

Steven stopped squeezing the toothpaste onto his toothbrush and stared at Genevieve in the bathroom mirror. "Thanks, honey," he said. "I don't have anything in mind for you to do for me."

"Okay." Genevieve picked up her eyeliner pencil and, as Anna had recommended, tried to highlight her eyes a little more dramatically. Her heart was light, and instead of feeling bombarded with frustration over Steven's leaving again, she felt thankful that he had been such a good and consistent financial provider. And she told him so.

Steven put down his toothbrush and turned to Genevieve, studying her closely. "What did you say?"

Genevieve turned to him with her freshly accentuated eyes. "I said I've never told you how much I appreciate that you've been a faithful and consistent financial provider for our family."

Steven didn't say anything.

"You've worked hard and long for years, Steven. I appreciate it. So do the girls. Because of your income, we've always lived in beautiful homes, and we've always had plenty of food and clothes and everything else we've wanted as a family. I just wanted to say thank you for providing for us."

"You're welcome." By the expression in Steven's sky blue eyes, Genevieve knew he was stunned. Returning to his toothbrush and toothpaste, he completed his task while he watched her out of the corner of his eye.

Inside, Genevieve felt sparkling. She felt pretty and

clean. She wanted to playfully splash a handful of water on her stunned husband to bring him back to reality.

But she didn't.

She quietly kept all her fresh feelings to herself. It seemed to her that if Steven was going to believe she was free, he would come to that conclusion naturally, based on her changed life and not on a few spontaneous actions.

Genevieve floated during the four days they had together before Steven left. She laughed, hugged her daughters, and smiled at Steven. He watched her carefully without asking questions.

On Sunday, the Ahrens family attended church. This was their third Sunday to file down the center aisle and sit in the middle pew on the left side. Nothing in the church had changed. The seat cushions were the same, the order of service was similar to the other two times, the stained glass window captured the summer sunshine and illuminated the front of the church with soft glimmers of broken light like translucent confetti. Pastor Allistar wore the same suit; Steven sat with his arm across the back of the pew and listened as he had the other times.

But for Genevieve everything was different. She was present. Completely present and involved in the service. Every word was for her. Each line of every song filled her up. She was like a playful kitten that had stopped scampering long enough to lap up milk from a saucer set out just for her.

The biggest surprise of all for Genevieve was the way she couldn't stop smiling. The biggest surprise for her family was the way she couldn't stop greeting people. On their other two visits to church, Genevieve had entered with her head down, barely shaking hands with the posted greeters at the doors. After church she had made a beeline down the aisle without acknowledging anyone and had gone directly to the car.

This morning, Genevieve was talking so much with so many people that Steven and the girls said they would wait for her in the car.

"You look beautiful today." Alissa gave Genevieve a hug in the parking lot. "How has the rest of this week been for you? I've been praying for you."

"I can tell. I've never felt so alive. My poor husband can't figure out what's going on with me."

"You should tell him."

"I thought if he saw the changes, he would know God had done something in my life."

"I think you should tell him what happened on Wednesday. You should say the words aloud to him. Tell him you unbound him, untied him. Let him know you don't hold anything against him. Tell him he's free. He might not know it yet."

"I was thinking of writing him a letter," Genevieve said. "After all our talking about God's letter to us and Jessica writing a letter to her dad, I thought I'd write Steven a letter this week while he is gone."

"I don't know. If it were I, I mean, if I were Steven, I'd want to know what was going on in your life by hearing your words and watching your face as you told me. Then you can write a bunch of mushy love letters all week long."

ROBIN JONES GUNN

Genevieve smiled. She was amazed that even though she guessed she was at least ten years older than Alissa, on a number of occasions, like now, she felt as if they were the same age. Alissa said once before that was because she had grown up so fast she had "an old heart." Genevieve believed that the two of them connected so well because they both had free hearts now.

"Thanks for your advice." Genevieve put her hand on Alissa's arm. "I'll talk to you later."

"Wednesday," Alissa said. "Two-thirty at Jessica's. And bring your girls."

"I will." Genevieve turned and walked with light steps to where Steven sat with the girls in the van, waiting for her. Before the sun set that day, she would make her confession to Steven, and then she would kiss him.

Her full lips curved up, just thinking about that kiss.

Chapter Fourteen

inner after church was tuna fish sandwiches and carrot sticks. Quick and easy. Genevieve sat down after she had placed the sandwiches on the kitchen table. "Steven, would you be interested in going for a drive this afternoon?"

"Okay. Any place in particular?"

"No, I thought it would be fun if we took your car. It's such a beautiful, sunny day. We can put down the top."

"Then we can't go," Mallory said. "What are we supposed to do?"

"You two can stay here or go over to a friend's house."

"I want to stay here," Anna said. "You two should have some fun for once. We don't mind staying here, do we, Mallory?"

"I guess not," Mallory said dejectedly.

Genevieve and Steven took off in the convertible, as

Anna and Mallory waved good-bye from the front steps.

"Mind if we stop by the café?" Steven asked.

Genevieve was surprised. "No. Why?"

"I haven't seen it since they knocked out the wall. I thought I'd have a look before I leave in the morning."

They entered through the front door, which Genevieve unlocked with a key. Underneath the door, on the floor, was a note.

Steven picked it up and read it aloud.

Genevieve,

   Well, the front of your café certainly impressed me. The flowerboxes and old bicycle are a nice touch. I was sorry to hear about the fire. Good for you for not giving up after such a loss. I'm glad to hear you're remodeling. It's too late for me to include you in this year's edition of Great Cafés of the Northwest, but I'll be back in the fall when I start work on my Great B and B's of the Northwest. I'll stop by for another omelet.

   Best wishes for your success,
   Richard Palmas

"Who is Richard Palmas?" Steven asked.

Genevieve told him about the writer who had challenged her to dazzle him when he was at the café last April.

Steven raised an eyebrow. "You sure he was challenging you to dazzle him with the café and your cooking?"

"Yes, of course."

"He wasn't trying to flirt with you?"

"Maybe a little." Genevieve gave Steven her full attention and a gentle smile. "But it didn't work if that's what he was trying to do. My heart is toward you, Steven, and no one else."

Steven looked as if he might believe her.

Genevieve knew this was the moment she had hoped would present itself on their drive. She was ready to open herself to him. "Steven, I have something to tell you. For a long time—our entire married life, in fact—I've harbored bitterness against you because of your career. You know that."

Steven tilted his head and pursed his lips together. He appeared ready to defend himself the way he had on numerous occasions.

"And," Genevieve said, holding up a hand to keep him from saying anything yet. "I was angry about the inheritance being lost, and I was hurt that your job takes you away so much of the time."

"Gena—"

"Let me finish. The reason I'm saying this is because everything has changed inside me. I finally saw that the bitterness and anger I held for so long was wrong. Very wrong. It was sin. Last Wednesday, while you were golfing, I went to Jessica's with Leah and Alissa. They were having a Bible study, and the girls and I stayed. God broke through to me that afternoon, and something happened inside me. I confessed my sin to God. I know He forgave me."

She drew in a breath for courage. "And I needed to forgive you, too. I know you never meant to hurt me with any of these things. I forgave you on Wednesday. I released you from the bitterness I'd wrapped you in. I untied you and let you go."

Evidently her words weren't having the effect on Steven she hoped for. With his chin out he said, "What do you mean you 'forgive me'? Are you saying I've done something wrong?"

Genevieve felt her mouth go dry. "That's how I perceived it."

"Did you have another flash encounter with God?" Steven asked. "When you went to that Bible study back in Pasadena, you came home talking like this about God forgiving you for all your sins and how I should get saved, too."

Genevieve nodded sheepishly. "Yes, I surrendered my life to Christ then. But I was still holding onto a tremendous amount of unforgiveness in my heart. It was choking me and keeping me in a dark and depressing place. On Wednesday I rolled the stone away from my heart, and I don't hold anything against you. I'm free. You're free. We can go on from here with a fresh start."

Steven was silent. He stopped looking at Genevieve and, with a furrowed brow, glanced around the café's interior, as if looking for something else to focus on.

I didn't say any of that the right way. I know what I mean. I know what happened in me. I can't explain it. God, please explain it to him. You make it clear because I can't.

"It looks like more foundational work is needed here than I realized," Steven said.

Genevieve wasn't sure if he was referring to the café or

to their marriage. Her voice was low as she said, "We can do it. It will be better than it ever was before. Sometimes when an important dream is demolished, it's so it can be rebuilt better and stronger."

Steven turned to his wife. "Do you really believe that?"

"Yes. For our marriage and for the café. Yes, I believe both of them will be better after they're rebuilt."

For a few moments they were silent. The faint scent of burnt wood and plastic tinged the air.

"Do you still want to go for a drive?" Steven asked.

"Yes. Do you?"

"Sure. Let's take a quick walk through here first."

Steven led the way into the new, open section of the café where the wall had come down.

Genevieve felt as if every step they took was a parallel to her life and their marriage. The wall had come down. The damage that had occurred wasn't repaired instantly, but the possibilities and opportunities for rebuilding were wonderful. Why was Steven having such a hard time seeing this as a liberating experience? He seemed to have bristled at her words about forgiving him. Did Steven think he had done nothing wrong in their marriage?

How could any father brush off that he didn't make it to the hospital in time to see his daughter's birth? Or think it wasn't painful for me to be at my mother's funeral alone? His excuse was always the same: work. It was his alibi. Doesn't he see the need to apologize to me even if his reason for missing all those important events was legitimate?

Genevieve realized she was heading down a path that

would lead her into darkness. She immediately stopped the bitter thoughts before they had a chance to embed themselves in her heart.

That's all in the past. It's forgiven. I'm free from the pain of those memories, and I choose not to hold it against Steven. It's his stuff now. He'll have to figure out what to do with it.

As they silently walked around the café's expanded interior, Genevieve remembered a conversation they had years ago when Steven said he had done nothing so bad that he needed a Savior to forgive him. The end result had been tears on Genevieve's part because she was a new Christian and had been trying to explain to Steven that he needed to surrender his life to the Lord.

Instead of sinking into a deep sadness or feeling responsible to educate Steven on every human's sinfulness and how every person had fallen short of what God desired to happen in his heart and life, she felt peace. All she could do was love her husband. That's what this next season of her life was about. She was free inside. Free to love this man that she had married, no matter what happened.

Exiting through the back door, Genevieve noticed the old metal chair that Anna had pulled from the storage shed last spring. It was tucked under a large cedar tree behind the café where it had sat for months, waiting for a fresh coat of paint and a new assignment.

Someone had placed a couple of glass vases on the chair. They were blue glass. Perhaps they had been a find yesterday at a garage sale Leah had visited. Shooting out of the top of the larger blue vase was a shock of wildflowers, almost spent for the season. Genevieve reached for one of the tall, blue bachelor buttons and twirled it between her fingers.

The poem from the framed, antique greeting card in Jessica's kitchen came to mind.

A single wildflower, given with love
Is better than
A dozen perfect roses
Given with indifference.

Genevieve turned to her husband. "I want you to know something, Steven."

He waited.

"I love you." The corners of her mouth curled into a generous smile. She held out the wildflower to him. "I love you. With all my heart, I love you."

Steven didn't move.

Genevieve knew it had been years since she had said those words to him. She had run their household with perfection while exhibiting indifference to her husband. Her small gesture of holding out the single wildflower was the widest, most loving thing she had done for him in a long time.

In that moment, Genevieve knew her heart was open to him. As open as it had ever been.

Steven took the flower from her. His expression softened. "I love you, too. I always have. I always will."

She tilted her chin toward him and drew close, inviting him to kiss her. Steven wrapped his arms around her and kissed her mouth as passionately as he had during the first weeks after they had met at Lake Zurich.

Genevieve returned the kiss with equal passion. In her mind's eye she stood on the edge of her towel on the grass at Lake Zurich, shivering slightly as the summer breeze dried the glistening droplets of water that clung to her skin. Before her stood Steven, fumbling for the right French word, pulling off his sunglasses and inviting Genevieve to soar into the endless blue of his admiring eyes.

They drew back. She opened her eyes and looked into the face of the first and only man she had ever loved.

"You meant that, didn't you?" Steven asked.

Genevieve nodded. "Yes, I meant it with all my heart. I love you."

Steven kissed her again, wrapping his arms around her and holding her as close as possible. "Gena," he whispered into her thick, brown-sugar hair. "My Genevieve."

What happened next was not planned. Steven and Genevieve locked up the café, returned to the car, and hit the open road with the top down. They communicated with loving expressions, snuggly hand holding, and spontaneous kisses at the stop signs.

They didn't talk about where they were going, but Genevieve guessed as soon as they roared under the curious gaze of the towering, friendly giants that lined the road to the coast. The trees weren't dripping with spring showers like they were the last time Steven and Genevieve drove past them. They didn't appear to be the solemn guardians of an enchanted forest. Today they were giddy bridesmaids, gathered in a row, waving and calling out for the bouquet to be tossed in their direction.

Genevieve laughed. Steven winked at her.

When they checked into the New Brighton Lodge, the clerk raised a knowing eyebrow when Steven signed the registration form and answered his question with, "No, we don't need a bellman to help with our luggage. Thanks anyway."

Steven and Genevieve walked away from the registration desk with their arms around each other, suppressing the laughter that Genevieve knew was gurgling up inside both of them.

As soon as they were alone in the elevator, Steven laughed. "Did you see his expression? He looked at us like we were a couple of middle-aged lovers sneaking off to start an affair."

Genevieve tilted her head and gave Steven's hand a squeeze. "Maybe we are."

He pulled her close and kissed her. Their lips stayed locked until the elevator door opened. Two young boys who looked like they were on their way to the pool, elbowed each other and smirked when they saw Steven and Genevieve wrapped in each other's arms.

Genevieve held in her surfacing giggles all the way to their room. Steven opened the door; Genevieve stepped inside. As soon as he put out the "Do not disturb" sign and closed the door, Genevieve laughed. Steven grinned broadly.

She felt young. Young and blissfully free.

Later that evening as they were driving home, Steven

summarized their spontaneous afternoon with simple words that made Genevieve cry. "I didn't think it would ever be like this for us again. You have no idea how much I love you, Gena."

The rest of the way home she rubbed his neck and hummed softly. The wildflower she had handed him earlier that afternoon was clipped to the underside of the visor. The fragile blue flower was protected from the wind as they roared past the row of now silent evergreens. Their gracious boughs seemed to be lifted heavenward in an attitude of reverence for evening prayers.

Genevieve found it easy to fill her thoughts with evening prayers and much thanksgiving.

When she and Steven pulled into the garage, the sun had just set. Mallory and Anna were sprawled on the sofa munching popcorn and watching a video.

"Did everything go okay while we were gone?" Genevieve asked.

"Um-hmm." Anna didn't take her eyes off the television.

"Were there any calls?" Steven asked.

"Fina called, and she wants you to call her back, Dad."

"And Leah called for Mom," Mallory added. "Remember?"

"Oh, yeah, Leah wants you to call her tonight. And we're out of milk."

Genevieve glanced at Steven. She wondered if he thought this reentry into everyday life seemed as out of place to him as it did to her.

How can it be that my life has changed so dramatically, and yet everything here is exactly as we left it?

But things weren't exactly the same. The first thing Steven did was to volunteer to buy milk for the girls for breakfast. It wasn't up to Genevieve to make life run smoothly.

"The grocery store will be closed," Genevieve said. "We can have eggs for breakfast."

"I'll make the eggs in the morning," Steven volunteered.

"Okay." Genevieve leaned over and gave her lover a kiss on the cheek. "I love you."

"I know." He took her in his arms and hugged her close.

Genevieve caught a glimpse of Anna and Mallory out of the corner of her eye. Both the girls had stopped watching the video and were watching Steven and Genevieve, as if caught in a moment of wonder to see their parents so snuggly.

Steven didn't let go and neither did Genevieve. They swayed slightly, moving to a gentle strain of music that no one could hear but the two of them.

"I'm going to miss you when I leave tomorrow," Steven whispered.

"I'm going to miss you, too."

"I wish I didn't have to go."

Genevieve could hardly believe her ears. Steven had never said that to her. "I wish you didn't have to go, either."

He kissed her neck. Shivers ran up her spine.

The phone rang, and Anna jumped to answer it. "I've got it!"

Steven and Genevieve slowly drew apart.

"It's for you, Dad. It's Fina."

Steven took the remote phone and headed for the living room.

Anna was staring with wide eyes at her mother. "Did you and Dad have a nice drive?"

"It was wonderful." Genevieve let her face take on the full smile that it wanted to carry at that moment.

"Where did you guys go?" Anna asked. "You were gone a long time."

"We went to the coast."

"Aww!" Mallory piped up. "I wish we could have gone. When do we get to go back to those tide pools?"

"I could take you girls sometime this week. We could take a picnic."

"I wish Dad could go with us," Anna said.

"So do I." Genevieve's words were honest yet they didn't carry any of the old barbs. "Maybe we can all go together in a couple of weeks when he gets back."

Anna seemed to still be examining her mother with her trademark scrutiny. "Mom, how come your shirt is inside out?"

Genevieve felt her face turn red. "It's not inside out, is it?" She pulled at the side of her sleeveless, blue knit top to have a look. Sure enough. The seam was on the outside. "How embarrassing. I must have worn it this way to church."

"It wasn't inside out at church," Anna said. "I would have noticed if it was."

Genevieve couldn't hide her blushing face from her daughters another minute. "I better turn it around." She hurried to the downstairs bathroom.

Closing the door, Genevieve looked at her red face in the mirror. She pressed her hands against her warm cheeks and looked into her sparkling gray eyes. Her hair was wind-blown from the ride. Dozens of wavy, sun-kissed strands had liberated themselves from the ponytail at the nape of her neck. They had positioned themselves around her face like a tangled cord of twinkle lights still hanging in there two weeks after Christmas.

Genevieve pursed her full, red lips together and com-manded the surge of embarrassed, delighted laughter to go back down. She swallowed it like ball of caramel taffy and felt the sweetness go inside her.

Oh, this is rich!

Genevieve slipped off her shirt and turned it around. She smoothed back her hair and smiled at her enlivened reflection.

This is so rich. Anna caught us!

A tiny giggle escaped from her mouth.

I am in love! Completely, wildly in love! And the man I'm falling in love with is my husband!

Chapter Fifteen

On Monday morning, Steven was late getting out the door.

He and Genevieve had fallen asleep in each other's arms, and when the alarm went off at 5 A.M., he had awakened his wife with kisses on her bare shoulder.

Steven was determined to make eggs for breakfast because he had said he would. Genevieve worked beside him in the kitchen, brewing a pot of his special coffee blend. This morning she added extra cinnamon just because everything about this man was extra spicy.

The girls weren't up yet when Steven reached for his travel coffee mug and kissed Genevieve good-bye. He kissed her and kissed her again. The expression on his face was one of agony as he touched her cheek with his free hand and gazed at her intently.

"I don't know what you've done to me," he said in a

deep voice. "But I hope I never recover."

Genevieve kissed his cheek and then his earlobe. She was about to whisper, "I forgave you. I released you. I untied you and let you go." But then she remembered how well those phrases had gone over the day before in the café.

Instead, she said simply, "God cleaned up my heart and flooded it with light." She kissed his neck. "And that's where I found something I thought I lost a long time ago…"

Steven pulled back and examined her expression.

"I found my love for you, and I'm not going to lose it again," she said.

Steven smiled at Genevieve. "I'll be back two weeks from tomorrow unless I can adjust my schedule."

"I'll be here waiting." Genevieve handed him his captain's hat. "Hurry home, my love."

"I will." He kissed her again before glancing at the clock on the wall. "Oh boy, I've got to fly."

Genevieve smiled at the pun. "Yes, you do. Bye."

"Bye. *Ciao, mon ami.*"

She stood in the middle of the kitchen wearing only her yellow fleece robe. Her skin still tingled from where his kisses had touched her that morning. Floating in the air was the subtle scent of his leather-toned aftershave mixed with cinnamon and French roast.

Instead of the old, sickening fears about their relationship as she drew in these mixed fragrances, a new, satisfying hope rose in her. *He'll be back. We'll have more wonderfully romantic times together. I have only begun to love my husband.*

Genevieve poured herself a cup of coffee and added

cream and sugar. She made herself comfortable in the rocking chair by the window that looked out on the backyard. Next to the rocker was her Bible. She opened to John 11 and read all the way through to the end of the book before she forced herself to pull away and take a shower. Leah was coming for breakfast at eight.

Dozens of questions, thoughts, and insights from what she had just read swam through her mind. She was glad that Leah was coming over. Genevieve didn't want to wait until Wednesday to discuss these questions with the other women at the Bible study, and Leah was always open to talking about God.

The part Genevieve wanted to discuss was in John 20 after Jesus was resurrected from the dead. He told His disciples that if they forgave anyone's sins, they would be forgiven, but if they retained anyone's sins they would be retained. Those were powerful words. Genevieve wanted to know more about what Jesus meant.

However, the discussion of spiritual matters didn't happen. The girls were both up and dressed by the time Leah arrived. Alissa had come a few minutes before Leah and was about to take Anna and Mallory swimming at the waterfalls near Camp Heather Brook. The girls had to go on a morning swim because the campers filled the lake area in the afternoon.

After Alissa and the girls left, Genevieve stuck a plate of the scrambled eggs Steven had made into the microwave and asked Leah if she wanted any toast.

"No, thanks. I'll get myself some juice, if that's okay."

"Sure, help yourself."

Leah placed a fat file folder on the kitchen table next to her plate of eggs, and as soon as Genevieve sat down, Leah jumped in. "This is what I wanted to show you—the plans for Glenbrooke Days." Leah's apple red cheeks glowed with excitement. "I've been talking to some of the older people around town, and you wouldn't believe how much they want to see this happen."

Leah pulled out a hand-written flyer and showed it to Genevieve. "We'll have a flyer like this made up profession-ally, of course, but this will give you an idea. The first Saturday in October looks like the best day. We'll close Main Street and bring back as many of the original events and booths as we can. It's going to be great!"

Genevieve was impressed to see the long list of partici-pants and potential contributors. "You're the head organizer, I take it."

"For the time being. If someone else wants to take over, I'll gladly let him or her have the whole project. But with extra time on my hands until the café is up and running, I can do this. Or at least get it started. And that brings me to my next point. We need to have the Wildflower Café in full swing by the first week of October. This is the biggest event of the year, and it will all happen right in front of the café. We must be in business by then."

Genevieve blinked. "That's only two and a half months away."

"I know."

"It's been almost two months since the fire, and you

know how much the builders have accomplished in all that time."

"That's why we have to get going!" Leah said. "And that's why I was so determined to meet with you first thing this morning. I don't know what it'll take, but as your new partner in business, I'm here to say we have to make a plan and push these guys to make the deadline. We have the money in the bank now, and all the legal papers have been completed. We can't waste a single minute."

Genevieve agreed with Leah. She didn't have quite the level of urgency that Leah did, but she certainly agreed with her in principle.

"The way I see it," Leah continued, "if you and I come up with a plan and meet with the builder to present our guidelines, then at least we're working with something. So far, you've been at his mercy, and he's been fitting you into his schedule whenever he pleases. The café needs to be switched from a sideline project to the top of his list."

Genevieve sat up straighter. "Okay, let's dive in. You know I'm not afraid of hard work."

For the next two hours, the two women put their heads together and their pencils to the papers in front of them. The list of ideas for how to design the café continued to grow. The options, now that they had double the floor space, were much broader.

Genevieve leaned back in her chair. "We have to narrow this down. We have to make some final decisions."

"I know," Leah said. "That's exactly what I've been saying. As I see it, we have two separate projects here. We have to decide if we want a normal little diner sort of café or if we want to do all these specialty areas like the tree house and the ice cream shop and the espresso cart."

"It's too much, isn't it?"

"It's just more complicated. We can do whatever we want. I like all the ideas, just as you do. But maybe we shouldn't try to do everything, or at least not right away."

Genevieve thought of her elaborate garden in Pasadena. It had taken years before she had all the paths and the bench, the swing, and the fountain exactly where she wanted them. When she had started to dream, she wanted it all. Every picture in every magazine captured her imagination, and she was certain she could make it all happen.

The process of sitting and picturing each section was what helped her the most. That, and the many years she worked on the garden. With the café, she didn't have time on her side.

"Come on," Genevieve said. "We need to go look at the café. We have to stare at the space for a while."

"What are you talking about?"

"I think we need to go to the open space and see it in our imaginations before we make a final decision."

With pens and paper, lists and folders, Genevieve and Leah drove to the café and parked in the back. Genevieve noticed the wildflowers in the vases on the chair under the tree.

"Did you leave those vases there?" she asked Leah.

"No."

"Are you sure? I thought it was a Glenbrooke Zorro sort of touch of beauty."

"Not this Zorro. It could have been Ida. She has a lot of those summer flowers growing like crazy in her side yard."

Genevieve picked up the vases and the now dried wildflowers and carried them into the café. To her they represented a new beginning, a touch of beauty in a place that had been desolate.

It brought a little smile to her face when she thought of how Steven had taken off for work that morning with the blue wildflower still clipped to his car's visor. Maybe he had glanced at it and remembered when Genevieve gave it to him yesterday with a wide-open heart.

Leah turned and looked at Genevieve. "How can you smile like that? Every time I come in here I still feel like crying."

"These two vases and especially these wildflowers mean something special to me. They represent a future full of promise."

"For I know the plans I have for you," Leah said.

"The plans *you* have for me?"

"No," Leah chuckled. "The plans God has for us. Haven't you heard that verse before? It's in Jeremiah. Chapter 29, I think. I learned it from one of Jessica's little index cards. You know, the cards she writes verses on so she can memorize them."

Genevieve didn't know Jessica wrote out verses on index cards, but she was curious about a verse that talked about plans that God made. "Do you know the verse by heart?"

"Yeah. It goes, '"For I know the plans I have for you," declares the LORD, "plans to prosper you and not to harm you, plans to give you hope and a future.'""

"I love that!" Genevieve said.

"Me, too. You know what I think?" Leah looked around the empty café. "I think we should pray. We should dedicate the rebuilding of this place to the Lord."

"Do you mean we should have a blessing party like Meredith and Shelly had for their parents' bed and breakfast when they wrote verses on the floors?"

Leah clapped her hands together. "Yes! Perfect! Let's do that. But for right now, let's pray. Just the two of us."

They stood in the center of the floor and joined hands. Leah prayed as naturally and openly as if Jesus were standing right next to them. Then she said, "Amen," and waited for Genevieve to pray.

Genevieve didn't jump right in. She knew what she wanted to say in her heart, but the words didn't tumble out of her mouth the way they had cascaded from Leah's mouth. Genevieve asked God to bless them and direct them as they made decisions about how to design the café. Then she added, "And be with Steven right now. Show him how real You are. Amen."

With renewed vision, Leah and Genevieve took what Leah called a "virtual" tour of the café, discussing all the options. They came to a conclusion that neither of them had expected: They had too much space.

For the cozy sort of dining they wanted, the openness and all the fun ideas like built-in trees were distractions.

Anthony, the builder, and two of his workers showed up at noon, ready to finish plastering the kitchen walls. Leah and Genevieve talked to him about their dilemma. Genevieve was feeling nervous about having purchased the other side of the building now that it appeared to be too much.

"Unless," Leah said, formulating aloud while sketching on a pad of paper, "we make some clever adjustments, like this." She turned the paper to Genevieve. "Expand the café this far into the new space, then put up a new wall, with a door of some kind between the two spaces. Then in this other, smaller area, we'll put in a special place for kids."

"What are you talking about? A daycare center?" Anthony asked.

"No, no, not a daycare center. A little ice cream shop. Or maybe a kids' bookstore that also sells candy and toys. What do you think?" Leah asked.

Genevieve wasn't sure. "How would we work that? It takes both of us to run the café. Who would run the kids' section?"

"I don't know. It would be separate. We could hire someone to run the store or hire a new person to wait tables."

"I don't know," Genevieve said. "It sounds like a lot more work."

"Not really," Anthony said. "I mean, as far as the restructuring. We could run a new wall six feet in from where the old wall divided the building. Once you decide what you want, I can get my whole team here, and we can have it up for you in no time. You just have to make up your minds."

Genevieve looked at Leah. Her eyes were lit up and her cheeks glowing.

"You know what?" Leah said. "This is what I want to do. I didn't know it until this moment, but I want to set up the shop for kids next door. Kids of all ages. I'll have a few toys for sale, Meredith can tell me what kids books I should stock, and I'll have ice cream. And hot cocoa in the winter. This is perfect!"

"Leah," Genevieve said cautiously, "are you sure you know what you're saying?"

Leah laughed aloud and clapped her hands together. "Yes! This is perfect! I'll call it the 'Dandelion'! Get it? The Wildflower and the Dandelion!" Leah spontaneously hugged Genevieve. "Seth is going to love this. This is so me. This is what I want to do."

Genevieve found it difficult to share Leah's enthusiasm. A few hours earlier, Leah was saying how jazzed she was about organizing Glenbrooke Days. Now she had launched into a blazing vision of a children's specialty store. Worst of all, Genevieve was losing her partner and the one who made the Wildflower a special place for the older customers. Genevieve could see them all leaving the café and gathering next door, exchanging their morning coffee for morning cocoa just to be near Leah.

"We need to talk about this and think this through." Genevieve looked from Anthony to Leah and back to Anthony. "I mean, this is crazy, Leah. You said this morning you wanted to have the café up by the first week of October, but now you're talking about a much more complicated plan. We would have to change the legal forms and file for new business licenses and—"

"We can do all that," Leah said. "Or more specifically, I can do all that. You can just concentrate on the café. It's your dream. Your baby. I need to be free to follow my dream, too."

Leah's words hit Genevieve hard. She was right. This was an old, familiar problem of Genevieve's. She had latched onto Steven when they were first married in such a way that she felt alienated and abandoned when she couldn't share his dream for flying. Once again, she had latched on to Leah and found it easy to depend on Leah to make her own dream a reality.

Genevieve needed to rebuild the café on her own. It was her dream. She knew that she needed to release Leah from their previous agreement to let Leah pursue her own dream. It was a painful lesson.

"Okay." Genevieve drew in a deep breath. "We'll be neighbors instead of partners. Would you like to call Collin and set up a meeting this week so we can change the papers?"

"Sure," Leah said. "I'll handle everything."

Anthony scratched his head. "When do you think you might have some direction for me?"

"Wednesday," Genevieve said. "Thursday at the latest. We have to get this show on the road."

All the mixed feelings that collided in Genevieve felt like a thick vegetable stew mushing around in her middle. She returned home and sat down with a fresh pad of paper. All the planning and changing and adjusting were exhausting.

Why is it, Lord, every time I pray about something, it falls apart? First, I prayed and said I wanted to be made well, and the fire breaks out. Now, Leah and I pray that You will direct us, and suddenly I'm without a partner, and she's starting a shop next door.

Genevieve realized not all the changes that occurred after she prayed were negative. The transformation in her relationship with Steven was wonderful. And it was certainly a change that came after a sincere prayer.

I guess I shouldn't complain, should I? Some people pray and say that nothing happens. I may not like what You're doing as You put my life in order, but at least something happens when I pray!

Chewing on the end of her pencil, Genevieve thought about how impossible all this was. If God truly knew the plans He had for her, He would have to make them clear because she was dumbfounded. And she told Him so in the longest prayer she ever remembered praying.

Anna and Mallory came in while Genevieve sat at the kitchen table with her hands folded and her head bowed.

"Mom, are you praying?" Mallory asked.

Genevieve paused midplea and looked up. "Yes."

"Is everything okay?" Anna asked.

"Yes. No. I don't know. Everything is changing with the café. I'm not sure what to do."

"Can we pray with you?" Mallory asked.

"Yes, of course. Please. Come here."

Anna and Mallory took seats on either side of Genevieve. They prayed for God to bless their mom, direct her, and show her what she should do with the café.

They were interrupted by the sound of the doorbell.

Anna jumped up to answer it and returned to the kitchen with a bouquet of bright summer flowers.

"They're for you." Anna handed the flowers to her mom.

Genevieve pulled the card out of the tiny envelope and read, "Gena, I miss you already. Love, Steven."

"Are they from Daddy?" Mallory asked.

"Yes." A smile came to Genevieve's lips. She pictured Steven arriving at a hotel room in Singapore sometime tomorrow. When he opened his luggage, he would find the love note she had quickly written to him that morning while he was in the shower.

Anna leaned close, as if trying to nonchalantly read the card before Genevieve could tuck it back into the florist envelope. "Mom, do you think God gave you back your love for Dad?"

Genevieve answered, "Yes. I think that's exactly what God did."

Anna sat a little straighter. "Well, if God can do that, then I think He can tell you what to do about the Wildflower Café. And I think He will, too."

"Me, too," Mallory echoed.

Genevieve nodded slowly. "Me, too."

The day before Steven returned home, Genevieve drove into Edgefield for a haircut. It was the first day in two weeks that she had been by herself other than to sleep at night. Anna and Mallory had both found great delight in entering into Genevieve's new plans for the café. They were with her every day and had assumed a sort of ownership of the café's changes. Anna particularly had entered in with gusto.

Leah had zoomed around for several days, pushing all the necessary details through the right channels at lightning speed. She and Seth had plenty of connections, and within one week of signing the papers for the Dandelion Corner, they had finalized the plans and ordered the necessary equipment, the first shipment of children's books, and some toys.

Genevieve hadn't moved at the same lightning pace, but she had come up with a floor plan she liked and asked Brad to help her order the necessary booths as well as tables and chairs from his source through the Internet.

Anthony made good on his promise and had a full crew there from morning till night once the plans were approved.

Thanks to Leah's forcefulness and relentless promotion of Glenbrooke Days, paperwork flew through the necessary town hall channels at record speed. Everyone knew Leah and was glad to help her.

With all the progress they had made during the past two weeks, Genevieve felt good about taking off for Edgefield that afternoon. Mallory and Anna were happy to stay behind and help Leah paint the interior walls of the Dandelion. Anna had come up with a sketch for Leah's back wall. It was a field of dandelions that were in what Mallory called "the wishing phase." That meant the slender green stems were topped with fuzzy white hats, all begging to be blown to the winds while some child closed her eyes and made a wish.

The plans for the Wildflower Café were less whimsical. Genevieve let the tree house idea go, but she held onto her wish for a fireplace. Brad helped her find a fireplace unit that could be installed directly up against the wall. It came with a wood mantle and, with the flip of a switch, could warm the area faster and more efficiently than any wood-burning fireplace. The best part was that it looked real.

The interior design was still taking shape. Genevieve was leaning toward a library décor with shelves and books. Her intent was to create an atmosphere that invited people to sit and feel comfortable. She thought she might substitute one of the table and chair sets with a love seat, two over-stuffed chairs, and a large coffee table in front of the fire. Guests might feel funny at first, dining off of a coffee table instead of at a booth. Her instinct told her it would catch on. All it would take was one cozy conversation by the fire with a bowl of her carrot and coriander soup, and customers would want to return a few days later to repeat the soothing experience.

Genevieve checked her watch when she pulled into the parking lot of the hair salon. Her appointment was at two o'clock, which was in five minutes. She hoped this didn't take too long because she wanted to do some shopping before she went home.

"What gorgeous, thick hair you have." The beautician lathered up Genevieve's hair. "How much did you want cut?"

"Not a lot," Genevieve told her. "I work at a restaurant, and I wear it back in a ponytail or up in a clip most of the time. It feels frazzled to me. I just want it freshened up and an inch or two shorter."

The beautician went to work, and when Genevieve

walked out forty-five minutes later, she felt lighter. Prettier. It was a good state of mind for her to be in for the next errand she had planned.

Genevieve drove to a nearby department store and headed for the lingerie department. It had been far too long since she had bought anything pretty for herself. Of all her wonderfully romantic memories, she cherished the sunny afternoon when Steven had whisked her off to the coast. The only regret she had was that her underwear was embarrassingly old. One of her straps had been held in place that afternoon with a small safety pin. It was definitely time to spend a little money on some new unmentionables.

Taking her time, Genevieve tried on a variety of undergarments. She decided to buy six pieces that made her feel feminine and attractive. She shook her head at a small stack of rejects that made her feel more like a freak of nature than a natural woman. It was the first time in her life that she remembered ever owning undergarments that actually matched each other and that fit her comfortably.

Maybe Steven would notice. Maybe he wouldn't. One thing was certain. Genevieve would know. And knowing that she had on pretty underwear and that her hair was shaped made her feel freshened all over. On impulse, she also bought a bottle of gardenia-scented hand lotion when she stopped for groceries on the way home.

Yes, Genevieve thought as she pulled into her driveway. *When Steven comes home tomorrow, he is going to find one fresh, feminine, and fragrant wife waiting!*

However, Steven didn't return the next day.

Chapter Sixteen

By eight o'clock Wednesday night, when Steven had neither arrived home nor called, Genevieve did something she hadn't done since the early days of their marriage because she disliked the procedure so much. She called the airline to check on his flight status. It usually took a minimum of half an hour for whoever answered the call to check the schedule and check the flights before he could make a rough estimate of where Steven was en route.

This time Genevieve found an automated system in place of a human voice. She checked the notes she had listed in the back of her address book and punched in the number for Steven's flight. The recording said the flight had arrived in San Francisco six hours ago. She then checked the numbers on the connecting flights that Steven usually took from San Francisco to Eugene, Oregon. If he made the first flight, he should have been home by six. If he was on the second flight, he would be home around nine.

Nine o'clock came and went. Genevieve took Steven's dinner out of the microwave and placed it in the refrigerator, covered with plastic wrap.

At ten o'clock, she sent the girls to bed, still trying to appear unconcerned.

At ten-fifteen, Genevieve called the airline again. This time she punched *O*, hoping an operator would come on the line. Instead, the automated service thanked her for calling and promptly disconnected the call.

This is what drives me crazy. This is what has always driven me crazy. Since Steven hates cell phones and refuses to wear a pager, I have no way to get ahold of him. He could be dead along the side of the road somewhere, and I wouldn't know.

She hit redial and listened to the list of automated options once again.

This does it. He has to get a pager. I can understand all his reasons for not wanting a cell phone, but there's no reason he can't carry a pager and simply turn it on when he's not flying.

Just then Genevieve heard Steven's Triumph sports car rumble into the garage. She slammed down the phone and flew to the garage, throwing her arms around Steven, as he emerged from the front seat.

"What's wrong?" Steven asked.

"I was so worried," Genevieve said. "Are you okay?"

"Of course. I'm fine." Steven held her at arm's length, examining her with a concerned look. "What got you so upset?"

Genevieve explained how she had called the airline and how helpless she felt when she couldn't get ahold of him. As she listened to herself, she remembered a time early in their marriage when she had gone through a meltdown like this when he was a day late in getting home because of flight delays, and he hadn't called her.

To steel herself against another such scene, Genevieve had told herself she didn't care. She had stopped paying attention to Steven's flight schedules. He came home when he came home. She didn't allow herself to keep track.

"I didn't know you would be so concerned." Steven stroked her hair. "I got the later flight out of SFO and did a little shopping in Eugene. I would have called if I'd known you would be so upset."

Genevieve shook her head. "I'm okay now. I thought you would be home sooner, that's all."

"Here, I bought these for you." Steven reached into the passenger's side of the car and pulled out a bouquet of daisies mixed with snapdragons. His smile showed that he hoped she would be pleased with his thoughtfulness.

"They're beautiful. Thank you." Genevieve gave him a kiss. They embraced and kissed again. Genevieve knew that if she didn't care deeply for her husband, she wouldn't have felt such a strong reaction. She saw it as evidence that her love for him was at a deeper level.

"I want you to get a pager," Genevieve said. "Or at least a cell phone that you keep in the car. I know we've talked about this before, but will you do this for me?"

"Sure," Steven murmured in her ear. "For you, anything.

Tell me what's been happening around here. What's the latest at the café?"

Genevieve had talked to Steven half a dozen times on the phone during the two weeks he was away. He knew all about the decision to divide the café and for Leah to start her own Dandelion Corner. The only part he didn't know about was the blessing party Leah had scheduled for Friday night. The walls were all painted so it was too late to write out Scripture verses on them, but the old linoleum flooring was being torn up at the end of the week. Leah thought they should gather a bunch of friends and have everyone write out favorite verses on the floor before the workers came in next week to lay the new flooring.

"So you're going to write Bible verses on the floor?" Steven said. "Isn't that kind of superstitious for Christians?"

"We're not doing it to ward off evil spirits," Genevieve explained. "Shelly's family had a party like this when they restored the Hidden House B and B. I heard Leah explain it as a way of leaving our mark on the building and getting us on our knees to pray at the same time."

Steven opened the Triumph's trunk and pulled out his wheeled suitcase along with a shopping bag. Genevieve followed him into the house, wondering what he thought of their blessing party and if there was any way he would join them.

"What time is the party?" he asked.

"Six o'clock. We're going to have pizza and then pass out the permanent markers." She knew it sounded strange. It still sounded strange to her, too, but she liked the idea of

marking the Wildflower as a place set apart. It meant something to her to ask for God's blessing on her business while
in a circle of close friends. If Steven didn't want to go with
her and the girls, she would understand.

"Do I get to pick my own verse?" Steven asked.

"Your own verse?"

"To write on the floor. Do I get to pick the verse I write
on the floor, or do you have them already selected?"

"No." Genevieve felt a spark of hope rise up inside of
her. "You can pick your own verse. I'm glad you want to
come."

"I wouldn't miss it."

Genevieve thought that was a remarkable statement.

Steven plopped the plastic shopping bag onto the
kitchen counter, and to her amazement, he pulled out a
modern translation of the Bible along with a tube of toothpaste, a can of shaving cream, and a box of his favorite
Mystic Mint cookies—the results of his shopping trip in
Eugene.

Tearing open the box of cookies, Steven said, "I thought
I'd buy myself a Bible. I'll find a good verse for your café,
Gena." Then, without missing a beat, he said, "Do we have
any milk?"

Over midnight milk and cookies, Genevieve and Steven
snuggled on the couch. He told her about another airline
that was going on strike and about one of his pilot friends
who had recently switched companies to work for the one
that was now on strike.

"I tried to tell him it was better to stay where he was,"

Steven said. "I told him I thought careers can be like marriages. We go through highs and lows, but it's better to stick it out in the lows and wait for the highs to return. He went from low to rock bottom, poor guy."

Genevieve licked the chocolate cookie crumbs off her thumb. "Steven, did you ever think of leaving our marriage when it was in one of its lows?"

He paused. "I thought about it. I guess everyone thinks about it. But I'm a man of my word. You know that. I don't know if it came from my father's military background or because my parents stayed together through all the highs and lows. I knew when you and I got married that we would stay married for life. For better or worse. Isn't that what we said in our vows? Do you want any more milk?"

Genevieve shook her head. Steven got up, and she was glad he hadn't asked her if she ever considered leaving their marriage. Over the years she had fleeting thoughts when she was really low. But she had abandoned the idea for their girls' sake.

Sitting there, with the cottage of her heart open and flooded with light, Genevieve made a disturbing realization. She may have never considered leaving her marriage by moving out and taking her share of the furniture, but that was exactly what she had done emotionally.

I divorced Steven silently on the inside years ago. I took my share of the interest and attention and directed it to other areas that I loved more.

The realization brought a sweeping sadness over her.

Oh, God, what did I do? I am so sorry. Please forgive me. I know You have forgiven me for my lack of forgiveness toward Steven and the way my heart turned cold and dark toward You and toward him. I just never understood until this moment that I had been living a lie in saying I was married when all those years I was really separated. Painfully separated from my husband. Forgive me, Father. You desire truth in the deepest parts of me. I don't want to ever live a lie again. Change me.

The sadness that had come over her passed the way summer clouds sail across the sky, covering the sun only long enough to make you look around and then look up to see if the darkened landscape is permanent. By then, the cloud has passed, and the sun returns unobstructed.

Genevieve knew God had heard. He had forgiven her. Again. The light still permeated her life. All was well.

Genevieve was grateful that when God began to heal her, He hadn't shown her all at once the places in her spirit that needed surgery. His healing hand was steady and gentle. Each incision of His scalpel had come at just the right time.

Steven returned with his glass of milk and sat beside her.

"Thank you," she said to her husband. "Thank you for never leaving our marriage, Steven."

Tears came as she tried to express all she was feeling. "I love you. I love you so much. It's like I was asleep for a long time, and now my heart is wide awake. I can't even begin to tell you how much I love you."

Steven sat back and soaked in her words with a contented expression on his face. "I know you love me. I didn't always know it, but I know it now. I think you know that I love you. I always have. I always will."

After a quiet twenty minutes of talking softly and expressing their hearts to each other, Steven and Genevieve went upstairs to their bedroom holding hands. Genevieve thought about the pretty new underwear she was wearing. She wondered if Steven would notice.

He did. Oh yes, without a doubt, he noticed.

Over the next few days, Steven noticed a lot of things. He commented on the way Genevieve was humming after she came home from her Wednesday afternoon Bible study at Jessica's. He noticed that she had planted some pansies in the neglected flowerbeds in the backyard. He also noticed that she had lost a few pounds.

"It must be all the exercise I'm getting while we're working on the café," Genevieve surmised when she stepped on the scale Thursday morning. "I haven't had time to eat much."

"You look great," he told her. "You've always looked great to me. Ever since you had your spiritual awakening or whatever you call it, you've gotten softer. You look lighter."

Genevieve thought his observation was amazing. She had thought that the night cream she had been using faithfully for the past five years had finally begun to live up to its advertising promises and was making some of her wrinkles disappear.

Steven's evaluation seemed more accurate. The wrinkles in her spirit had disappeared, and the results could be seen on the outside. Genevieve wondered why no one had ever advertised forgiveness as the best beauty aid around.

If Genevieve had thought any of these insights would

make sense to Steven, she would have shared them. But she didn't know what he was taking in lately and what he was brushing off as he had for years.

Steven went golfing again with Pastor Allistar on Thursday and came home saying that he "admired" Gordon Allistar. That didn't seem to indicate any spiritual revelations had occurred on the greens.

On Friday morning, Genevieve got up at seven-thirty and found Steven was up already, mowing the backyard. She guessed he was tackling the chore while the day was still cool since the prediction for this first week of August was for a string of scorchers. His dislike for yard work made the lawn mowing a labor of love, which Genevieve reminded herself to comment on. She wasn't in the habit of telling Steven how much she appreciated everything he did when he was home.

By the time she had showered, slipped into her coolest cotton dress, and tucked her hair up in a clip, Genevieve was aware of the morning's warmth. She opened all the upstairs windows and woke up Mallory in the process.

"Do we have to get up now?" Mallory asked.

"No, you can sleep in if you want to, honey."

"You smell good, Mom."

Genevieve kissed her freckle-faced angel and caught a whiff of pool chlorine in Mallory's hair.

Genevieve went downstairs and grabbed her sandals, which she had left by the front door. After Steven's comment about her being "softer," she had tried an old beauty trick of slathering her feet with thick cream last night. Then, pulling on socks over her creamed feet, Genevieve padded around the house in her moccasins, feeling the cream squish between her toes.

The results were wonderful. This morning the feet she slid into her summer sandals were smooth and happy feet.

"Good morning!" she called to Steven from the door that opened to the backyard.

He cut the motor on the lawn mower and came over to where she stood in the morning sunlight, looking and smelling as fresh as a daisy. Steven hadn't shaved. His T-shirt was darkened by perspiration. His shorts and hairy legs were dotted with clippings, which had been cut off from their patch of green earth.

"I'd kiss you," Steven said, "but I'm a slob at the moment."

"That doesn't matter to me." Genevieve opened her arms, offering her affection.

"No," Steven said. "I'll save up a good one for you after I get cleaned up."

"I'll be waiting," Genevieve said.

A peculiar look came over Steven's face. Genevieve couldn't make it out because she faced the brilliant morning sun and Steven was in the shadows.

"Are you okay?" Genevieve asked.

Steven ran his hand over the top of his head. "You…I…"

Genevieve thought he looked upset. She couldn't imagine how anything she said could have sounded negative to him.

"Have you ever heard Gordon tell how he met his wife?" Steven asked.

"No." Genevieve had no idea what that had to do with Steven's getting rattled. Why would her comment on how she would be waiting for him to kiss her after he got cleaned up be disturbing? It wasn't like her husband to lose his cool the way he seemed to have.

"You'll have to ask them about the airplane incident sometime," Steven said. "I'm, ah…I'm going to get back to the yard."

Genevieve made a ham and cheese quiche for breakfast and watched Steven finish up the yard work. He appeared to be deep in thought.

The phone rang. The builder was calling to say that a delivery truck was at the café and that Genevieve was to go over and sign for the shipment.

"I have to go to the café." Genevieve called to Steven out the window.

He cut the motor again and looked up. "When will you be back?"

She thought for a fraction of a second how that had been her line for the first twenty years of their marriage. "I'm not sure. Call me or come by later. A delivery truck is there now, and the driver is waiting for my signature. I left a quiche warming in the oven."

"Okay," Steven said. "Why don't you take the Triumph in case I need to drive the girls some place in the van?" He waved, and she scooted out the door.

The PDS truck driver was unloading the last of a twenty-box shipment of new dishes. Genevieve signed the form and cut open the first box.

"What did you get?" one of the construction workers asked.

"Really adorable dishes." Genevieve grinned broadly. "They are exactly what I wanted. Look at them! The colors are perfect! Don't you love the wildflowers around the edges?"

The toughened construction worker adjusted his tool belt. "I guess. Oh, wait. I get it. Wildflowers. That's the name of your place, right?"

"Right." Genevieve chuckled. "The Wildflower Café." It seemed to her at that moment that the previous Wildflower Café had never existed. It was a shadow of what this new, vastly improved café was going to be. In some ways, she saw the same thing happening with her marriage. Everything was new and fresh.

The cupboards in the kitchen had been finished for almost a week. Genevieve had coaxed Anna to wipe out all the construction dust a few days ago. Now, with glee, Genevieve unpacked her new dishes, washed each one by hand and lovingly stacked them in her new cupboards. Everything fit exactly the way she had planned.

That night, when the group gathered for the blessing party, Genevieve pulled Alissa aside and took her into the kitchen. "I know I'm going to sound like a little girl playing house, but I had to show someone my new dishes. Look at these." She pulled out a plate and handed it to Alissa.

"Oh, I love it! What do the bowls look like?"

Genevieve opened the adjoining cupboard and lifted out a bowl. "Aren't they adorable? I've never been silly about plates or silverware or any of that. I get more excited about a really nice frying pan. But these are such an improvement over the generic white ones I inherited from the Wallflower Café."

"I don't even remember what those looked like," Alissa said. "Except that every bowl I ever had soup from was chipped. I used to think they gave me the same bowl every time, but then Brad ordered soup, too, and we both ate out of chipped bowls."

They admired the matching salad plates, and Alissa said, "You should use a set of these plates somehow in decorating. You could hang a plate on the wall or put one on a stand inside the bookcase that you're going to put by the fireplace."

"Great idea," Genevieve said. "When I get to that stage in a week or two, would you come over and give me some ideas?"

"Sure. I'm not especially creative in that area, though. Jessica is the one who has an eye for taking classical looks and making them fresh. Or you could ask Lauren. She's the pro when it comes to fixing up old furniture, you know."

"Maybe all the women from our Wednesday group could come for the day and help me bring this place alive."

"Yes! You know all of us would love it."

Three-year-old Beth trotted over to where Alissa stood beside the sink and tugged on her mom's shorts. "Mama, pizza! Come eat."

"Well!" Genevieve said. "That sounded like a couple of complete sentences to me."

"Yes, both girls have learned to say 'pizza' and 'come eat.'

They pick up new words every day. It's amazing to watch. Once they understood that this was their new life, they started to blossom."

"Here." Genevieve handed Alissa a stack of wildflower plates. "Let's eat our pizza on these. I couldn't bear to serve any of my guests off paper plates when I have these honeys stacked up and waiting in the cupboard."

Alissa laughed, and the two of them carried the plates in to the group gathered in the hollowed-out cavern of the dining room. The lights had been installed that day. They were energy efficient bulbs covered with shades that were of a creamy, golden hue. They hung from the ceiling at what appeared to be random points, but were actually carefully planned so that each light would hang over a separate table.

Three of the booths were installed next to the window. The back of each booth seat was a tall divider made of wood and filled in with stained glass at head level. The fourth booth wasn't finished yet. It was the largest booth. The shape was rounded, and it was tucked in the far right corner. The wooden bench seats for the larger booth had been completed that afternoon but no comfortable cushion softened the seating yet. The table hadn't been installed either.

A single, shaded light hung from the ceiling above the corner booth, casting a golden glow on Steven, who sat beneath it with his head down. All the other guests were collected at the table in the booth next to the door.

Genevieve set down the plates and went over to her husband who sat alone, reading in the unfinished corner booth.

"Are you ready for some pizza?" she asked.

Steven looked up with an expression of wonder on his clean-shaven face. In his hands, he held the Bible he had bought for himself.

Chapter Seventeen

W hat did you ask me?" Steven looked up from the corner booth.

"Are you hungry? The pizza is ready." Genevieve noticed that the others had linked hands in a circle and were praying.

"You go ahead and join the others. I'm trying to find my verse to write on your floor."

Genevieve's heart warmed. "Have you found one?"

"Not yet. I only made it halfway through." Steven held up the Bible and showed where he had stuck a broken rubber band as a bookmarker in the third chapter of Zechariah.

"Why are you reading Zechariah?" If Genevieve had known Steven was reading his Bible, she would have directed him to the New Testament. He could have been reading John along with her. That would have prompted some interesting discussions.

"I'm reading Zechariah because that's as far as I got," Steven said. "I started reading on Wednesday, but I'm only halfway through."

"You're reading the whole thing?" Genevieve was stunned. She knew her husband was a fast reader, but she didn't know anyone who had sat down and read the entire Bible.

"Of course. Haven't you read the whole Bible?"

"No." In all the years Genevieve had been a Christian, she had read little of the Bible. The only parts she took the time to read were the sections being discussed in Bible study groups. At this moment she wished she had read the whole Bible. She wished she had put aside other things that had snatched away her time over the years. She had no good reason for having failed to read through the Bible at least once.

"It's a pretty amazing book," Steven said. "I'm not saying I understand all of it, but I definitely see a reoccurring theme."

Genevieve nodded, waiting for Steven to tell her the insight he had discovered. Before Steven could, Gordon stepped over next to Genevieve. "Here ya' go, Gena. The hostess should have the first slice, I always say."

"Thanks." She took the plate he held out to her and showed Steven. "How do you like my new wildflower plates?"

"Nice. And that's a good looking pizza, too."

"We just happen to have a slice with your name on it," Gordon said. "You wait right here, and I'll bring it to ya'."

"You better not look too experienced at waiting tables,"

Steven called out to Gordon. "Gena happens to be looking for someone to replace Leah. She might hire you, if the preaching thing doesn't work out."

Genevieve wasn't sure how to take her husband's jesting. She quickly looked to Leah, who stood a few feet away, and then at Gordon, who was in the middle of the rest of the group.

"Now you've got a winner of an idea there," Gordon said, unruffled by Steven's comment. "I've even got experience as a waiter. Did you know that? I would love to come in here on my day off and wait tables. What do you think, Teri?"

Gordon's wife, Teri, didn't get a chance to comment. At that moment, Gordon turned with a plate of pizza and bumped into the edge of the booth. He lost his balance and appeared to be trying not to collide with Brad and Alissa's youngest, who had plopped down in the middle of the floor with her plate of pizza in her lap.

With his arms flying into the air, Gordon tilted to the side, caught himself, but lost the plate of pizza. It soared across the room like a Frisbee and landed with a crash on the floor next to where the fireplace was to be installed.

The room went silent. All Genevieve saw were the broken pieces of her beautiful wildflower plate smashed on the bare floor. Ami burst into tears and held up her arms for Alissa to take her. No one spoke.

"It's okay." Genevieve drew in a breath of courage. "I'll clean it up."

"I take back my suggestion that you start working here,

Gordo," Steven said. "Stick to the preaching."

Gordon apologized to Genevieve. She swept up the broken pieces and saved them in a small box under the kitchen sink. The plate was in too many pieces to glue back together, but she couldn't throw it away.

Returning to the party, Genevieve told herself it was a good thing her husband was on such friendly terms with the pastor and that they were ribbing each other like buddies. The others were teasing Gordon as well, saying that everyone was fortunate he had a strong wooden pulpit between him and the congregation when he preached on Sundays. At least the pulpit could break his fall and protect the people in the front row if he had a clumsy spell in the middle of a sermon.

The broken plate was soon forgotten. The pizza was soon devoured. The marking pens were distributed, and the blessing party went into full swing.

Genevieve knew what she wanted to write on the floor. She had found the verse at the end of the book of John during her recent reading. Getting on her knees by the front door, she drew a rectangle like a large welcome mat. Inside the rectangle she wrote,

"Jesus saith unto them, 'Come and dine.' John 21:12."

That small part of the last chapter of John had jumped out at her because she understood more fully than ever what it meant to hear Jesus' voice and to respond to His kind invitation. She wanted everyone who entered this café to feel invited and to find a deeper level of friendship, as they gathered around a warm fire or with a cold glass of lemonade.

Jesus had invited His closest friends to "come and dine" around a small fire on the beach. She wanted her friends to know they were welcome to "come and dine" at this café.

She finished her welcome mat with a few flowers in the corners and then walked around, eager to see what the others were writing.

Anna had created a darling outline of a house that Mallory was helping her decorate with curls of smoke from the chimney. In the center of the house, Anna wrote:

"This is My commandment, that you love one another. John 15:12."

Teri and Gordon were kneeling in front of the booths where Teri was writing, "Oh, taste and see that the Lord is good."

Their twin boys were lying flat on their stomachs, coloring a picture of a beach scene compete with palm trees and whales jumping in the curling waves. Little Malia slept in a baby carrier, blissfully unaware of all the activity around her.

Leah leaned against Seth. She had just begun to write on the floor by the opening that separated the Dandelion from the Wildflower.

A Dutch door had been installed so that the two businesses could close off their sections from the other if they wanted. The door could be locked if they needed it to be, or it could have the top closed while the bottom stayed open, inviting short visitors to enter. The other option was for the door's bottom section to be closed while leaving the top open.

"We already wrote our favorite Zephaniah verse on the

floor in there," Leah said, nodding into her new Dandelion Corner. "Can you guess what verse we're going to write here?"

Genevieve took a guess. "Is it the verse you told me about the other day? The one that refers to how God knows the plans He has for us?"

"Exactly." Leah flipped her silky, summer-blond hair behind her ear. "Jeremiah 29:11."

Shelly and Jonathan couldn't come because they were swamped with the large group they had at Camp Heather Brook that week. Friday nights were always their biggest night because all the campers gathered in the outdoor amphitheater after the sun went down. They sang under the stars and campers told what God had done in their lives that week. Shelly had said more than once at their Wednesday Bible study that it was her favorite time of the week.

Since Shelly and Jonathan couldn't join the pizza party, they had sent their blessing via Alissa. Shelly's sister, Meredith, had e-mailed a verse to Alissa and asked her to include it on the floor for her and Jacob.

"This one is from Shelly." Alissa pointed to where she had written out, "Sing to God, sing praises to his name; lift up a song to him who rides upon the clouds. Psalm 68:4."

"And this one is from Meri and Jake." Brad put the finishing touches on his stick letters. In all caps he had written, "DEEP CALLS TO DEEP IN THE ROAR OF YOUR WATER-FALLS. Psalm 42:7."

Lauren had gathered Alissa's daughters along with her daughter, Molly Sue, and Jessica's two daughters. The five little girls were barefooted and giggling as Lauren drew around their feet. They were scattered around the room, frozen in place until Lauren traced their feet. Then they hopped to a new location and froze, waiting for Lauren to come trace more footprints.

It kept the little ones involved without letting them loose with a bunch of permanent markers. Lauren's husband, Kenton, was holding their son, Michael, and helping to direct the little foot models. Kenton had written beneath the first set of footprints, "Ephesians 5:8, Walk as children of light."

Genevieve loved it. She knew that every time she trotted from the kitchen into the dining area, she would remember that beneath the flooring were dozens of miniature footprints and the reminder to always walk in the light.

Jessica and Kyle were kneeling by the entrance to the kitchen. Jessica was helping their precocious five-year-old son draw a picture of a building on fire and a stick figure fireman putting out the flames with a shooting fire hose.

Kyle was writing, "He has sent me. . .to give them beauty for ashes, the oil of joy for mourning, the garment of praise for the spirit of heaviness. Isaiah 61:3."

Genevieve began to choke up. God had done exactly that. He was giving her beauty for ashes and joy for her mourning. And more than anything, she felt as if she had exchanged a spirit of heaviness for a new life of praise.

"Thank you," she whispered to Kyle and Jessica.

Jessica looked up and smiled. Genevieve noticed in the direct lighting that Jessica had a scar in the shape of a half moon above her right lip. Genevieve wondered if this quiet woman, who appeared so at home on her knees, also knew a little bit about beauty and ashes.

Only one person remained whose artistic endeavors Genevieve hadn't viewed yet. Steven.

Genevieve gingerly approached the corner booth where her husband knelt on the floor. He held his new Bible in one hand and a black permanent marker in the other.

"This is it," Steven said to her. "This is all of it, right here."

Genevieve couldn't imagine what he meant. Steven hadn't written anything yet. She saw that his Bible was turned to Zechariah 13.

Standing beside him, Genevieve watched as Steven wrote, "They will call on My name, and I will answer them; I will say, 'They are My people,' and they will say, 'The LORD is my God.'"

Steven looked up at Genevieve. "I get it. This is it."

Genevieve didn't get it at all. She considered calling Gordon over to this private alcove. If Steven was about to comment on some deep spiritual truth, he would want to discuss it with a pastor, wouldn't he? Especially if he was wanting to debate some obscure point in a part of the Bible Genevieve had never read.

Steven didn't debate. He didn't make any profound comment. He didn't even speak. All he did was reach for Genevieve's hand and draw her down to the floor where she knelt beside him. He bowed his head and held her hand tightly.

Is he praying? Is my husband praying? Or is he waiting for me to say something? Does he want me to pray? What is happening?

Genevieve knelt in silence while the sounds of their friends echoed around them. The barefooted little girls were still giggling; Josiah corrected his twin brother on how whales held their breath underwater; Leah called across to Anna and asked if she had any more blue pens. The rest of the room, the rest of the world continued to whirl in an unaltered orbit.

But in this tiny corner of the world, this secluded corner of the café, all of life seemed to have stopped. Genevieve closed her eyes and prayed for her husband like she had never prayed before. Somehow she knew at this moment her husband was calling out to God. With all her heart, she begged God to answer him.

Steven's grip on Genevieve's hand suddenly let up. She fluttered open her eyelids and turned to look at him. For more than two and a half decades she had watched his face but never had she seen this expression before. He wore his surprise like a banner across his broad forehead. A glow like the steady embers of a campfire lit his eyes. His lips were pressed together, and his jaw was tipped upward, setting his face like a flint toward the verse he had just written on the floor.

"This is it," he said in slow, even words.

"This is what?" Genevieve knew something powerful had happened inside her husband, but she couldn't discern what it was.

Steven drew in a deep breath. His nostrils flared. Pointing at the words on the floor he said, "I called on God."

Genevieve still didn't know what to make of all this. Steven, her calm, steady husband, wasn't following any pattern of logic that she recognized. If he had just surrendered his life to the Lord, it certainly wasn't the same way Genevieve had turned her life over to Christ.

"Steven," she said softly, "I don't understand what you're saying."

He looked at her with a calm, almost humored expression. "You don't?"

Genevieve shook her head.

Steven took both her hands in his and kissed them. "It all made sense to me." He got up off his knees and drew Genevieve up with him. He sat on the bench, and she sat beside him, the two of them tucked in their private alcove while the rest of the guests splashed their artistic blessings all over the floor and continued the party in the Dandelion Corner.

"I saw a repeating theme as I was reading the Bible. God wants His people back."

Genevieve nodded. She had never heard the entire Bible reduced to such a simple theme before, but in a general sense, that was what she understood to be the essence of God's redemptive message.

"I never understood that we're separated from God. He wants us to come to Him, but we're a mess." Steven shrugged and smiled at Genevieve. "That's why God sacrificed His Son. That's how we can come to God. Through Christ only."

Genevieve nodded again. Steven had it all figured out. "How did you get all that?"

"From you. You released something deep in me when you forgave me, Gena. I'm sure of it. This morning, do you remember how you held out your arms to me while I was working in the yard?"

"Yes."

"You looked so beautiful, fresh, and clean with the light in your hair and your arms open. I wanted to go to you and embrace you, but I couldn't come close because I was such a mess. That's when I started to get it. I always thought I was good enough to come to God because I'm a pretty decent, hard-working fellow. But all that hard work only made me sweaty and dirty."

Genevieve smiled. He was pretty smelly this morning.

"Gordo told me the last time we went golfing that when he first proposed to Teri, she turned him down and boarded an airplane. He told her he would wait for her, and he did. He stood right where he had left her, waiting. Teri actually made them stop the taxiing plane so she could get off. When she entered the terminal, Gordo was standing right there, waiting for her."

"I hadn't heard their story before," Genevieve said.

"Gordo compared that to the way God waits for each of us to come back to Him."

Steven reached over and touched Genevieve's face. "The reason I was so taken with you this morning was because you said you would wait for me, just like Gordo's example of how God has been waiting for me. All day I've been thinking that it was time to stop this plane, so to speak, and get right with God."

"And is that what happened when you were kneeling just now?" Genevieve asked.

"Yes." His voice was steady and sure. "I called on God. I asked Him to forgive me. I know He did, Gena." With a nod of his head, Steven said, "I'm one of His people. He is now my God."

The tears chased each other down Genevieve's cheeks. Her pulse pounded in her ears.

Jesus, You just resurrected my husband, didn't You? You gave him new life. You told me to untie him, and look what happened. I let him go, and he went right to You. This is a miracle!

"I am so, so happy," Genevieve whispered.

Steven leaned over and kissed away her tears before they made it all the way down her face. "Now what?" he asked.

"I don't know," Genevieve said. "Do you want to say something? I mean, every person in this room will be ecstatic when they find out. You might as well tell them all at once."

Steven gazed into Genevieve's eyes. "Stand with me, okay?"

"Always," Genevieve said.

Hand in hand, Steven and Genevieve moved to the center of the café. All across the floor were dozens of nimble footprints, artistic flowers, and verses of blessing. Genevieve noticed that she was standing on the word "love" from Anna's verse. It was the most obvious command God had ever given her to do, and yet she realized now how poorly she had obeyed it. She had loved others sparingly over the years. That would change. With all that had happened in her life and the opportunity to daily invite people to come and dine in this café, that would change.

"Can everyone hear me?" Steven asked in a loud voice.

The guests at the blessing party turned their attention toward Steven and Genevieve who stood, hand in hand, heart in heart, looking as if they had an important announcement to make. Jessica helped to quiet the little children.

Gordon quipped, "You two look like you're about to announce your engagement."

"They're already married," Mallory said with her hand on her hip. Then with a look of great hope she asked, "Are you pregnant, Mom?"

All the adults laughed. Mallory failed to see why that was so funny. She went over to Genevieve and stood beside her, wrapping her arm around her mother's waist and leaning her head on Genevieve's arm. Not to be left out of the family moment, Anna slid over next to Steven and slipped her hand into his free hand, as if she were in the know about her dad's mysterious announcement.

"I'm sure my wife would like to say thank you to all of you for coming and putting your blessing on this café," Steven said.

Genevieve looked at him and then glanced at their friends. "Yes, thank you. All of you. This has been, well…it's been an exceptional night."

"It has," Steven agreed. "I don't know any other way to say this, but, ah…I, um…well. When I got on my knees over there, God met me in that corner, and He finally got ahold of my heart." Steven's voice caught on the last word.

Genevieve noticed he was blinking away tears.

The room fell silent.

"I don't even know the proper term to say, but I wanted all of you to know that tonight I came to Christ. Or maybe I'm supposed to say Christ came into me. All I know is that I believe. God is now my God. I am one of His people."

Gordon let out a wild, whooping cheer and punched his fist into the air. Anna and Mallory threw their arms around their father, and the rest of the group smothered him with cheers, tears, and praise.

Genevieve heard little Travis yelling over the noise, "What happened? What happened?"

Mallory told him, "My dad just became a Christian tonight! He's going to be in heaven with us!"

Whether he understood or not, Genevieve watched as Travis started to dance around in a little circle, singing a lively praise song he probably learned at church. Mallory knew the song and sang with him. She joined hands with Travis, and the two of them danced as they sang.

What happened next was beyond anything Genevieve had ever expected. The room filled with singing, laughing, and dancing. She couldn't stop laughing and crying at the same time.

Gordon gave her a big hug and shouted over the singing, "Just imagine what the angels are doing right now in heaven! God says that when one sinner repents, the angels in heaven rejoice."

Genevieve pictured Pastor Allistar standing in front of the stained glass window at church making this booming proclamation. An exquisite sort of power came from a beautiful picture that had been formed out of shattered pieces of glass. It was the same way now, in her life. She thought of the breathtaking image of the gentle lamb that Jesus held in His arms in that beautiful window. Steven was that lamb. Jesus had called to him and called to him. And now the good Shepherd had him back, right where He always wanted Steven to be. Safe in His everlasting arms.

Chapter Eighteen

On the first Saturday in October, Genevieve forced her feet out of bed when the alarm went off at six. She coaxed herself into the hot shower and let the warm water pelt her back, hoping it would release her sore muscles. All of the last-minute demands of Glenbrooke Days, coupled with today's grand reopening of the Wildflower Café, had left her with only four hours sleep.

What I need is a dose of Steven's espresso beans. Or at least two beans—one to hold up each eyelid.

Cutting her relaxing shower short, Genevieve pulled on her yellow robe and scurried downstairs. The house was quiet.

On the counter, the coffeemaker was keeping a pot of coffee warm. It had been sitting there since five o'clock when Genevieve ground up the decaf espresso beans and added the French roast with three dashes of cinnamon. Steven had come down the stairs, fresh from his shower, right on time. He thanked her for the coffee, kissed her soundly, and left for the airport.

That's when Genevieve sneaked back into bed for an extra bit of sleep. That little luxury had pushed her behind schedule. Waking the girls, she told them to get some breakfast before they left the house at seven.

"Can't we eat at the café?" Mallory moaned.

"No, the café won't open until after the parade. We have a lot to do in the next few hours to get everything ready. So I want you to try to eat something before we leave here."

Genevieve sipped her coffee and went to the closet. The new, white cotton blouse she had purchased for this important day hung on a hanger next to a comfortable pair of black pants. She had decided on going for basics and accessorizing with a special scarf that had belonged to her mother. The scarf was typical Swiss. The background was a soft cream color, and splashed across it were dainty white Edelweiss flowers, yellow buttercups, bright blue cornflowers, and delicate red poppies.

Rolling up the sleeves on her crisp white blouse, Genevieve smiled as she dressed. She vigorously brushed her thick, brown-sugar hair, then took her mother's scarf, folded it in a triangle, and twisted it until it formed a narrow headband. Genevieve wrapped the scarf around her head and secured it underneath her hair in the back with a tight knot. The results were as she had hoped. Her hair would be kept out of her eyes, and the scarf brought color to her face.

Memories of her mother were sweet this morning, as were memories of her father.

You told me to make something of my life that would shine brightly, Dad. Genevieve gazed at her reflection in the mirror. *And do you know what I discovered? Creating anything that will shine brightly is impossible without God. It's even more impossible without a clean heart.*

Genevieve smoothed a few dots of sheer lotion over her clean face and put on enough makeup to camouflage the puffiness around her sleepy eyes. She made good use of her eyeliner and twisted open a new tube of lipstick.

"Did you know," she pursed her lips to blend the color and talked softly, as if her stern father were standing behind her. "I think there *is* something in my life that shines brightly."

Genevieve grinned. "It's me. I shine brightly. Not because I'm so great but because God has done something amazing in my life. He brought the light inside."

"Mom?" Anna called from the entrance to Genevieve's bedroom. "Mom, who are you talking to?"

"No one," Genevieve answered quickly. "What do you want, honey?"

"Do you think it's going to be warm enough to wear shorts?"

"It's up to you," Genevieve said. "You can always bring a change of clothes with you. Whatever you decide on, move quickly. I'd like to leave in about fifteen minutes, if not sooner."

Anna was ready in ten minutes, with a stuffed gym bag

flung over her shoulder. She had braided her hair in two short braids that skimmed her collarbone. Tucked in the fold of the hair fasteners that held her braids were two yellow daisies.

"Do you think my hair looks too silly like this?"

"No, I think it's adorable. What about you, though? What do you think?"

"It's okay, I guess. Alissa said I should wear it like this so that, when I paint the kids' faces at our booth, they will think I'm fun."

"Oh, you *are* fun." Genevieve wrapped her arms around Anna.

"No, you're fun," Anna countered.

Anna had turned fifteen two weeks ago, and they had celebrated at the coast with five of her girlfriends. Genevieve had used some of Steven's travel discounts and had reserved a suite for one night at the New Brighton Lodge. Genevieve, Anna, and Anna's five girlfriends packed into the van and spent two days laughing, eating, beachcombing, and telling stories.

During that birthday weekend, Genevieve saw how fun her artistic Anna could be. Also during that weekend, on the drive home while the other girls slept in the back of the van, Anna had reached over from the front passenger's seat and had given her mom's arm a squeeze.

"I don't know if I ever told you this before," Anna said, "but you're a great mom. You're really fun to be around."

"No, you're fun," Genevieve had countered.

"No, you're the one who's fun," Anna teased back.

They had bantered in the car for several minutes until one of the girls in the back seat hollered, "You're both fun, okay? Now can you let the rest of us get some sleep here?"

Genevieve now stood with her arm around her middle daughter and gave Anna's daisy-decorated braid a playful tug. "No, no, *you're* fun."

"Okay," Anna quipped. "We're going to be late so this time I win. I'm the funnest."

"Funnest what?" Mallory called from the kitchen.

"Nothing," Anna told her. "It's just a game we were playing."

"You were playing a game?" Mallory said. "I thought we had to leave."

"We do!" Genevieve pulled Anna down the stairs with her. "We have to leave right now. Are you ready, Mallory?"

"I've been ready!"

Genevieve gave her youngest a hug and a warm snuggle. "You are the best."

"The best what?"

"The best at being ready this morning. Come on, we have lots to do."

The three of them drove down a side street and wound around the block to park behind the Wildflower Café. The back door to the kitchen was open, and Leah was tossing out an empty cardboard box.

"The dairy order finally arrived," Leah said. "You must have been getting nervous."

"I wasn't nervous yet." Genevieve joined Leah in the sparkling new kitchen. "But I was getting there."

"I can help you put the rest of this away if you want me to." Leah had on a navy blue "Glenbrooke Days" sweatshirt, jeans, and well-worn tennis shoes.

"The girls and I can do this," Genevieve said. "You must have a thousand other things to take care of about now."

"Actually, everything is running as smooth as can be," Leah said. "It helped setting up the booths and getting the road blocked off last night. A few of the people who are selling crafts and things are finishing putting their booths together now, but everything else is good to go. The weather sure turned out nice, didn't it?"

"Gorgeous," Genevieve said.

"I think I'll change into my shorts." Anna slid past Genevieve and headed for the refurbished bathroom.

Genevieve reached for one of her new Wildflower Café aprons and draped it over her head. It was light blue-and-white pinstriped with a bouquet of bright flowers appliquéd on the bib. She had ordered four of them, including, as a surprise, a smaller one for Mallory.

"I better wear an apron, too," Mallory said, exactly as Genevieve predicted she would.

"Not one of those," Genevieve said.

Mallory's face fell. "Do I have to wear one of the old, stained, white ones? I thought all those got burned up in the fire."

"No, you have to wear this one." Genevieve pulled open a side drawer and lifted out a junior-sized Wildflower apron with the initials "MJA" embroidered under the bouquet of flowers.

Mallory's eyes grew wide. "For me?"

"Yes, for you, Mallory Janiece Ahrens. Your very own apron."

"Mom, this is so cool! Thank you!"

"You're welcome." Genevieve eagerly received Mallory's hug. Kissing Mallory on the cheek, she said, "Let me tie it on for you."

The apron was a perfect fit and a big hit. Genevieve felt as if everything was going to fall in place today, just the way it was supposed to.

"Hey," Leah said while unloading a box of cartons of milk, "I heard he was coming today after all."

Genevieve turned around. "Steven?"

"No, Richard Palmas. Did you hear he cancelled his stay at the Hidden House last weekend, but when he heard about Glenbrooke Days, he said he would come today after all. I wouldn't be surprised if he didn't turn out to be one of our first guests when we open the door."

Genevieve looked through the small arched window that now connected the kitchen to the dining area. "I wonder what he'll have to say about our little café now?"

Leah closed the refrigerator and walked over to Genevieve. She put her arm around Genevieve's shoulder and said, "I'm sure that this time he'll be dazzled."

"Mom?" Anna stepped out of the restroom in a different outfit. Her two braids had turned into two high pigtails with the daisies now stuck into the ponytail holders at the crown of her head. Instead of shorts, she had on a short skirt, sandals, and a long-sleeved black sweater with beaded fringe along the bottom.

Leah, Mallory, and Anna all paused to take in the outfit. It wasn't the best combination Genevieve had ever seen, but she wasn't worried. They had an hour and fifty-two minutes before they opened their front door. Anna would most likely change outfits at least once before then.

"Mom," Anna said, "do you want me to put the flowers in the vases now and put a vase on each table?"

"Yes, please."

The two blue vases that Genevieve had found weeks ago on the chair under the cedar tree out back had been, as Leah had suspected, gifts from Ida. Genevieve liked the cobalt blue so much that she had Lauren hunt up another dozen vases. Some were bright yellow, some green, some red. They were all different shapes, but all were made of dense glass. Today the flowers were a mixture of the end-of-the-season wildflowers that Leah had collected all over town the day before from generous supporters of the Wildflower Café.

Anna went to work, doing what she did best, making little bits of beauty. Mallory helped Genevieve and Leah put the frosting on the dessert of the day, Meri's Midnight Madness Chocolate Cake. They also were serving Shelly's Snickerdoodles all day long.

"When did you want to pop the chicken in the oven?" Leah asked.

Genevieve had made up eight pans of Alissa's Ritzy Chicken the night before and had them all waiting in the refrigerator. Her beautiful new oven could take four of the large pans at a time. "I'm glad you asked. We should get the first four in now because it will be a little late for breakfast when we open. Some people might be ready for more sub-stantial food by then."

"Are you opening the Dandelion Corner at nine o'clock, too?" Mallory asked.

"No, we're going to open at eight-thirty," Leah said. "How would you like to be the one to help me cut the rib-bon?"

"Really?"

"Yes, really. Seth is over there now getting the cash reg-ister stocked."

Genevieve set the oven to preheat for the chicken and pulled out a pot for Jessica's Broccoli Cheese soup. "How do you think your new assistant is going to work out?"

"Tracy is a gem. She's going to be great. She loves kids, and now that her oldest son just started middle school, she was eager to find a part-time job. It's ideal for both of us."

Leah had gotten the idea in her head that she could run the Dandelion Corner as well as wait on customers at the café during the breakfast and lunch rushes. She claimed that her vision for the Dandelion Corner was more along the lines of starting up the store. Her heart was really more with the older folks who would be coming to the café and not the children's shop.

After a long discussion a week ago, Leah and Genevieve had agreed that things could go back to the way they were before the fire as long as Leah hired someone to work at the Dandelion, kept a timecard for her work at the café, and allowed Genevieve to pay her for the hours she waited tables. It was an unusual setup, but it seemed like the easiest way for everyone to get what was best all around.

"To be honest with you," Leah said, "I think everything about our new arrangement has God's fingerprints all over it."

"I do, too," Genevieve said. "And it certainly has a mass of children's footprints all over it."

Leah didn't appear to catch Genevieve's meaning. Genevieve nodded toward the dining area. She was referring to the outlining Lauren had done of the children's feet at their blessing party. All the footprints and verses were now secretly tucked under a fabulous new flooring. They would remain hidden there until someday, when someone else with a dream would own this building and transform it into whatever he or she envisioned.

Genevieve whispered a thank-you to God for the hundredth time. She still couldn't believe her dream was coming true. In little more than an hour they would unlock the front door, and the Wildflower Café would be reborn.

"Mom," Anna called from the dining room, "what do you think? Come see."

Genevieve walked through the alcove opening to the dining room that was angled at a slant with the new bathroom door so that diners couldn't see into the kitchen. She stepped into the beautiful dining area and felt her heart swell with thanks all over again. To her right was the new wall, partially covered with bookshelves stacked with a variety of books, all available for customers to borrow and enjoy while at the café. Two of Anna's hand-painted, framed pictures hung on the wall next to the charming Dutch door that was open on top at the moment, revealing Seth as he stood inside the Dandelion, frantically blowing up balloons with a helium tank.

"Would you like some help?" Genevieve asked him.

"Sure," Seth said. "Anybody over there available?"

"I'll help," Anna said. With a wave of her hand toward Genevieve she added, "Tell me what you think of the vases. Too many flowers in them? Or do you like them?"

"I love them," Genevieve said quickly. "Just the way they are. You did a fantastic job."

Anna opened the Dutch door, looking like a rather tall fairytale character entering a fanciful cottage.

Genevieve took in another sweeping view of the café. The new tables were light oak with a thick-coated sheen on the top, making them safe from spills. At each table the colorful glass vases held their portion of wildflowers. They were all different yet lovely. They reminded Genevieve of her variety of friends in this quaint corner of the globe. All the women in Glenbrooke were different yet lovely in their own way. All of them caught the light, the way the glass vases did. All of them cast a glimmering beauty wherever they went.

Out the front windows, Genevieve could see the warm, autumn-toned mums that lined the window flowerboxes along with a few fat, orange pumpkins perched in the corners for added color.

In front of the flowerboxes sat the card table Anna and Alissa had set up the night before as their face-painting attraction. When Genevieve and the girls had strolled down Main Street last night, she was surprised to see the variety of booths. The people of Glenbrooke had come out in full force to support Glenbrooke Days and had responded generously when Leah asked them to be involved. The booths offered everything from Genevieve's fudge to handmade log cabin birdhouses.

The new booths inside the café offered comfy bench seats and excellent views of the parade and all the other happenings that would monopolize Main Street today. The corner booth on the far right side, which Leah and Genevieve had come to call "the prayer closet," already had been the quiet corner for conversations, last-minute planning, and, of course, the sacred memories of Steven's prayer.

The café's original front door remained intact in the far left corner next to the front windows. However, Mack from the hardware store had taken it down, sanded it, and refinished it two weeks ago. It was ready to open and close a hundred thousand times without registering a single complaint.

The far left wall, which was the first thing visitors saw when they walked through the café's door, was the fireplace. Above the mantle, Genevieve had hung a mosaic picture she was especially proud of. Anna had helped her design and set a single flower in plaster of Paris. The flower was made from bits of the first wildflower dish that Gordon had broken the night of the blessing party.

Unable to throw it away that night, Genevieve had saved it in a box under the sink. A few days later, when the kitchen was finished, she found it and remembered how one of the women in her Bible study had said that some things need to be broken first before they can be used best.

This particular broken wildflower plate was definitely being used best. It was set apart from all the other dishes that would be used everyday at the tables. This broken plate was now the crowning touch above the fireplace.

Beside the mosaic picture was a small, framed antique greeting card that Jessica had given Genevieve two days ago as an early café warming present. The sentiment on the picture, which had come from Jessica's kitchen, matched the broken wildflower plate mosaic perfectly.

A single wildflower given with love
Is better than
A dozen perfect roses
Given with indifference.

Genevieve liked the fireplace. She liked the way the grouping around it had turned out. Two high-backed, cozy chairs faced each other on either side of the hearth, and a love seat faced the flame. Between the love seat and the fireplace sat a long, low table on which Anna had placed the largest of the original blue vases brimming with wildflowers. It looked exactly as Genevieve had envisioned it. Warm. Inviting. Rich. And deliciously comfortable.

She thought of the verse she had written on the welcome mat by the front door. "Jesus saith unto them, 'Come and dine.'"

Yes, Lord Jesus, that's exactly what I want to happen here. I want people—Your people—to always know that they can come to You and come to this café, and dine with You and with Your people. I completely surrender this café to You, just as I have completely surrendered my life to You. Fill it with light, just as You did my life. Make it shine for You.

"Gena," Leah called from the kitchen, "we have a slight problem."

Genevieve trotted back in the kitchen and saw Mallory with a ring of chocolate frosting around her mouth.

"I haven't started the soup yet," Leah said. "But it's after eight already, and I need to help Seth. I told Mallory she could come help me. Sorry to leave you in the lurch like this."

"That's okay. Mallory, honey, wash your face. I'll take it from here, Leah. You've done more than enough. Thank you. I'll get all this going, and then I'll step over to watch you cut the ribbon at eight-thirty."

Genevieve quickly went to work. At eight-thirty she hurried over to the Dutch door. Standing there with the bottom of the door closed and the top open, she watched Mallory as she helped Leah cut a wide yellow ribbon across the front door.

A cheer went up as dozens of people, young and old, entered the Dandelion Corner. A line immediately formed at the ice cream counter. The twins ran to examine the low table with the windup toys and big yellow trucks. Lauren's daughter, three-year-old Molly Sue, made a beeline for one of the big beanbag chairs where her older cousin, Emma, joined her. The two girls giggled and tapped their feet together.

Travis went for the books. Beth and Ami went for Mallory and Anna.

From all indications, it was a grand success. Genevieve turned back to the kitchen, first making sure that the bottom of the Dutch door was locked so she wouldn't receive any early guests.

"You're not trying to keep business away, are you?" a deep voice asked.

Genevieve looked up and saw Richard Palmas standing on the other side of the Dutch door, his green eyes taking in everything he could.

"Hello," Genevieve said. "How are you?"

"Can't complain. And you?"

"Great. I'm doing great."

"It looks like it," Richard said. "You look ten years younger than the last time I saw you. I'm impressed, after all you've been through. What's your secret?"

"Love," Genevieve said without hesitating.

"Anyone I know?"

"My husband," Genevieve said.

Richard's face registered his surprise. "Well, that's a twist."

"I have to get back to the kitchen," Genevieve said. "We'll be opening the café at nine."

"Great. I'm ready for a good omelet."

Genevieve smiled. "For a good omelet, you came to the right place."

She returned to the kitchen humming. She found Jessica standing in the kitchen beside an older man dressed in a knit shirt that bore the logo of an expensive designer line of sportswear. For a moment, Genevieve thought the man might be an inspector of some sort.

"Gena, I hope you don't mind us slipping into the kitchen like this," Jessica said. "I wanted to catch you before the café opened and everything turned into a mad rush for you."

"You're welcome in here anytime, Jessica. Front door, back door, it doesn't matter to me."

If the man with Jessica was an inspector, Genevieve might have violated some health regulation by stating that Jessica could enter the kitchen at any time.

But he wasn't an inspector.

"I want you to meet my father," Jessica said. Her smile lit up her face.

Genevieve froze in place. Another walking, breathing miracle was standing inside her café. Mr. Morgan's being here meant he had responded to Jessica's letter. By the look on Jessica's face, their relationship had been restored.

"It's a pleasure to meet you, Ms. Ahrens. Jessica has told me about your rebuilding efforts, and I wish you great success."

"Thank you." Genevieve shook his strong hand. "It's wonderful to have you here today, Mr. Morgan. I hope you'll have time to join us for breakfast. I make a fairly commendable omelet."

"That sounds good to me. I promised my grandkids I'd watch the parade with them first, though." His stern face took on a softness when he said, "my grandkids."

Jessica beamed. She slipped her arm through her dad's as they left and said with a wink over her shoulder, "We'll be back later."

Genevieve couldn't stop humming.

At five minutes to nine, all the pieces were in place. Leah entered through the back door. "Is this great or what? You met Jessica's dad, didn't you? Isn't that incredible? He arrived yesterday afternoon, out of the blue. God is doing amazing things around here. I love it! I'll wash up and put on an apron. You better get out there and unlock the door before the crowd knocks it down."

Genevieve felt her heart pounding as she took each step toward the door. This was her dream. This very moment. This was the reoccurring scene in the dream she kept having months ago in which the phone rings and Steven tells her he's stuck in Chicago.

Not this time.

Genevieve scanned the crowd of familiar, smiling faces outside the window searching for her husband. But Steven wasn't there.

Go ahead. Unlock the door.

Just as she reached for the doorknob, Genevieve heard the stomp, stomp and patter, patter of footsteps behind her. She turned to see the man she loved. His steady eyes were as blue as Lake Zurich on a summer's day. Beside him was their firstborn daughter, Josephina.

"Mom!" Fina cried, as she wrapped her arms around Genevieve and plastered a kiss on her cheek. "I'm so glad you and Dad sent me a ticket and told me I had to come. This is awesome! Look at this place."

Genevieve kissed Fina on both cheeks. "Look at you. You're beautiful."

"So are you, Mom. You look great. Doesn't she look great, Dad?"

Steven's eyes twinkled. "Yes, she does."

"I'm so glad you're here." Genevieve reached for Steven's hand and gave it a squeeze. "Both of you. This means a lot to me."

"Are you kidding?" Fina flipped her long hair over her shoulder. "I'm the one who's glad to be here. Dad drove like a maniac all the way from the airport because my flight came in late. He was determined we get here on time."

Steven drew his wife close. He kissed her tenderly and whispered, "I wouldn't have missed this for the world."

And Genevieve believed him.

Dear Reader,

Why is it that wildflowers give a sense of fresh starts and renewed delights? Is it the way they spring up along the side of the road and seem so carefree and independent? Wildflowers aren't carefully planned and planted in rows. They appear where least expected. They surprise us with their color. They amaze us with their bright beauty.

Wildflowers, however, are also fragile.

Maybe that's what got me thinking about Genevieve and her creative, colorful spirit. She was supposed to have a walk-on part in Glenbrooke 4, *Sunsets*. But I kept thinking about her. I wondered if she was really as vibrant and free as she appeared to be at first glance. That's why I wanted to write a story about her. I wanted to understand the fragile side of Genevieve's wildflower spirit and watch her blossom when the Son flooded her life with light.

While I was working on this book, I visited my parents. It's been over five years since a stroke paralyzed my dad. Mom still cares for him at home. She is my hero.

On their coffee table I noticed an old book titled *Wildflowers of North America*. My grandpa gave the book to my grandma in 1963 when they celebrated their thirty-fifth wedding anniversary. On the inside cover, Grandpa penned a sweet poem to his wife.

May the beauty of each flower portray
A vision of my love so true
As each and every flower portrays to me
The blessing I have received from you.

I copied his words in my journal, wondering what it would be like to be married for thirty-five years and to be told that after all that time I was still a blessing to my husband. I want to love and be loved with that same brightness and whimsical clarity.

My parents just celebrated their forty-eighth anniversary. I thought about all the wildflower days that have sprung up during the past five years for them. Days that were not carefully planned and planted in rows. Fragile, wildflower days that in the randomness of their appearing brought unexpected brightness and color to the depth of my parents' love.

With this story comes a prayer for all of you who are in a wildflower season in your marriage. May God show you where any roots of bitterness and unforgivingness have begun to grow in your heart. May His only Son, the Great Healer and Patient Gardener, remove those deadly roots from your life completely. And may the Holy Spirit send a fresh breath across the garden of your heart, releasing the fragrance of His beauty and scattering His seeds of new beginnings. May all your days be wildflower days—fragile and fragrant. Carefree and bright. Filled with light and love.

Always,

Robin Jones Gunn

P. S. You are invited to come visit me online at www.robingunn.com

Now that our oldest son is in college, it's rare for us to be together, let alone all sit down to dinner together. A few months ago, we were all in southern California at the same time. We gathered at the home of some special friends—John and Debbie. Debbie and I went to high school together. We double-dated in college. We had our first babies in the same hospital with the same doctor. Our husbands bought dune buggies together and took them out racing in the desert. Then our family moved, and for many years our only regular communication with John and Debbie and their growing family was through Christmas cards.

When we sat around John and Debbie's dinner table a few months ago, our grown children gazed at one another shyly across the table. "Do you boys remember going to swimming lessons together?" Debbie and I asked them. No. They were only four at the time. "Do you girls remember playing together at the beach?" No. They were only pigtailed toddlers.

Then my son took a bite of Debbie's chicken, and a familiar look floated across his face. "Hey, now I remember this!" he said, digging in for another bite. "Mom, how come you never make chicken like this?"

Debbie and I exchanged the ageless look of women who should know by now that the way to a man's heart is through his stomach. "I'll give you the recipe," Debbie whispered. "There's nothing low-cal about it, but trust me. Your kids will ask for it every time they know you're going to cook for them."

Sure enough. I'm leaving for a book-signing trip this

Wednesday. I will be at my son's apartment in Florida for a total of thirty-two hours before flying to Atlanta. "Is there anything you'd like me to bring?" I asked on the phone last night. At first he said no. Then he paused and said, "Is there any chance you could make some of that good chicken while you're here?"

In honor of my long-time friend Debbie, and with love to starving college sons everywhere, here's the recipe for:

ALISSA'S RITZY CHICKEN

4 boneless, skinless chicken breasts
1 can of cream of chicken soup
1 strip of Ritz crackers, crushed
1 cube of butter, melted
$1/2$ cup of sour cream added to the top, optional

Place chicken in casserole baking pan. Cover with soup. Top with crushed crackers, and pour melted butter over the top. Add sour cream, if desired. Bake at 350 degrees for 45 minutes.

THE GLENBROOKE SERIES

by Robin Jones Gunn

COME TO GLENBROOKE...

A QUIET PLACE WHERE SOULS ARE REFRESHED

Imagine a circle of friends who enter into each other's lives during that poignant season when love comes their way. Imagine the sweetness of having those friends to depend on as the journey into marriage and motherhood begins.

Meet the women of Glenbrooke: Jessica, Teri, Lauren, Alissa, Shelly, Meredith, Leah, and Genevieve. When their lives intersect in this small town, the door to friendship is opened and hearts come in to stay.

Perfectly crafted, heartwarming, and rich in truth, Robin's Glenbrooke novels have delighted half a million readers with their insights and charm. All souls looking to be refreshed are warmly invited to come to Glenbrooke.

SECRETS
Glenbrooke Series #1
Beginning her new life in a small Oregon town, high school English teacher Jessica Morgan tries desperately to hide the details of her past.

1-57673-420-X

WHISPERS
Glenbrooke Series #2
Teri went to Maui hoping to start a relationship with one special man. But romance becomes much more complicated when she finds herself pursued by three.

1-57673-327-0

ECHOES
Glenbrooke Series #3
Lauren Phillips "connects" on the Internet with a man known only as "K.C." Is she willing to risk everything...including another broken heart?

1-57673-648-2

SUNSETS
Glenbrooke Series #4
Alissa loves her new job as a Pasadena travel agent. Will an abrupt meeting with a stranger in an espresso shop leave her feeling that all men are like the one she's been hurt by recently?

1-57673-558-3

CLOUDS
Glenbrooke Series #5
After Shelly Graham and her old boyfriend cross paths in Germany, both must face the truth about their feelings.

1-57673-619-9

WATERFALLS
Glenbrooke Series #6
Meri thinks she's finally met the man of her dreams...until she finds out he's movie star Jacob Wilde, promptly puts her foot in her mouth, and ruins everything.

1-57673-488-9

WOODLANDS
Glenbrooke Series #7
Leah Hudson has the gift of giving, but questions her own motives, and God's purposes, when she meets a man she prays will love her just for herself.

1-57673-503-6

WILDFLOWERS
Glenbrooke Series #8
Genevieve Ahrens has invested lots of time and money in renovating the Wildflowers Café. Now her heart needs the same attention.

1-57673-631-8

Sisterchick n.: a friend who shares the deepest wonders of your heart, loves you like a sister, and provides a reality check when you're being a brat.

SISTERCHICKS ON THE LOOSE!
Zany antics abound when best friends Sharon and Penny take off on a midlife adventure to Finland, returning home with a new view of God and a new zest for life.

ISBN 1-59052-198-6

SISTERCHICKS DO THE HULA!
You can't cancel an adventure you've dreamed of for this long... An unexpected pregnancy only multiplies Waikiki's wackiness for two middle-aged Sisterchicks who are dying to let their hair down.

ISBN 1-59052-226-5

SISTERCHICKS IN SOMBREROS!
Coming October 2004
Two Canadian sisters inherit beachfront property in Mexico and take off on an adventure to claim their inheritance. With the help of a few locals, the Canadian cuties figure out what to do with their less-than-desirable legacy.

ISBN 1-59052-229-X